THE MAGIC DOG

*The
MAGIC
DOG

I. G. EDMONDS

LODESTAR BOOKS
E. P. Dutton   New York

LIBRARY OF CONGRESS CATALOGING IN PUBLICATION DATA

Edmonds, I. G.
    The magic dog.

SUMMARY: Traces the career of the magician known as the Great Lafayette and his partner, an extraordinary dog named Beauty.
    1. Neuberger, Sigmund—Juvenile literature. 2. Magicians—Biography—Juvenile literature. 3. Dogs—Training—Juvenile literature. 4. Conjuring—Juvenile literature. [1. Neuberger, Sigmund. 2. Magicians. 3. Dogs—Training. 4. Magic tricks] I. Title.
GV1545.N48E35   793.8′092′4   [B]   [92]   82-4991
ISBN 0-525-66757-1   AACR2

Published in the United States by E. P. Dutton, Inc.,
2 Park Avenue, New York, N.Y. 10016
Published simultaneously in Canada by Clarke, Irwin & Company Limited,
Toronto and Vancouver
Editor: Virginia Buckley   Designer: Trish Parcell
Printed in the U.S.A.   First Edition
10 9 8 7 6 5 4 3 2 1

Contents

1 * A Most Unusual Dog

BEAUTY LOOKED LIKE an ordinary dog. But she was not. She was one of the most unusual dogs that ever lived. Beauty—and this is the truth—was a magician! The Great Lafayette, who was Beauty's stage partner, said so.

Beauty was a small, short dog with floppy ears. She had white hair, and a large brown spot covered one eye. She looked like some kind of hound, but nobody ever knew what breed she was. The Great Lafayette, who was not always the most truthful man, said she was a "gheckhound," from the island of Gheck. If this was true, then she was the world's only gheckhound. Nobody else had ever heard of such an animal—or such an island—before or since.

Although it is questionable what kind of dog Beauty was, there is no doubt about her having been a magician. We find accounts of her in histories of stage magic, in old newspapers, and in stories told by those who saw her. They all agree that the dog *was* a magician.

I first heard of Beauty from a man named Felix Marshal, who saw Beauty perform. This was in 1950, when Felix was sixty years old. He saw Beauty do magic tricks when he was eleven, so that would have been in 1901. Vaudeville was then a very popular form of entertainment. The usual vaudeville bill presented a number of different acts. Along with the singers, dancers, jugglers, and acrobats, the show often included a magician.

It was at such a vaudeville show that Felix Marshal saw Beauty, the dog magician.

"My mother did not approve of vaudeville," Felix told me. "In those days women wore skirts that touched the ground. Mother thought the girl dancers showed too much of their ankles on stage.

"So she said No when I asked her to take me. I cried, argued, and pleaded. I had never seen a magician in my life, and I wanted to see this one, who called himself The Great Lafayette, so badly that I even agreed to study extra hard and improve my school marks. Finally she agreed.

"Though I had never seen a magician, I had a friend who had. He told me about the show he had seen, so I thought I knew what to expect. But oh, was I wrong! What I saw was more wondrous than anything I had ever dreamed of seeing. What made this show so marvelous was Beauty the dog."

What Felix saw Beauty do was indeed wondrous.

2

2 * A Strange Magician

THERE WERE EIGHT acts in the show that Felix Marshal saw. The boy sat impatiently through a song by a male singer. He was disappointed when the second act was a dance by six girls. This was followed by a troupe of acrobats.

An usher came onstage between each act. He changed a card on an easel at one side of the stage. This announced the next act in the show. Felix almost yelled in excitement when the card read:

THE GREAT LAFAYETTE AND BEAUTY

His excitement turned to disappointment. The curtains parted on an empty stage. There was no magician at all. There was a small table with a chair beside it and an overturned box on the stage, but nothing else. The cardboard box had neither top nor bottom. It lay on its side, and the audience could see through it.

"Where's the magician?" Felix asked his mother.

"Be quiet!" she said in an angry whisper. "You're disturbing the other people."

A small boy in front of Felix asked his father the same question. The man chuckled and said, "Maybe he made *himself* disappear!"

Some show, Felix thought. We've been gypped.

Then a small dog came trotting from the wings. Felix sat up with increased interest. The dog went to the overturned box. She pushed it over with her nose. It fell with the open bottom against the stage floor. Now the audience could see only its sides.

The dog turned and went to the table. She jumped up in the chair so she could reach the tabletop. She picked up a small black stick in her mouth. It was a magician's wand. The dog jumped from the chair and trotted back to the box. She sat up on her hind legs and shook her head to wave the wand.

Felix's mouth flew open in surprise as a man rose out of the *empty* box.

"I *knew* it was empty," Felix told me. "I saw through it before the dog nosed it over. So *where* did the man come from? I asked my mother. She was so surprised herself that she forgot to tell me to be quiet."

The man rising from the empty box wore a dress suit, top hat, and rimless glasses. He did not look at the audience, but tipped his hat to the dog. She dropped the wand from her mouth and barked at him.

The man looked startled. He glanced at the audience

for the first time. He seemed surprised to see the people there. He tipped his hat to the dog again.

"I'm sorry I interrupted," he said.

The man dropped back out of sight into the box. The dog came over. She stood on her hind legs, putting her forepaws on the edge of the box. Her weight caused it to tip, almost turning over. This let the audience see under the box. It was empty again. The man in the top hat had vanished!

Felix was amazed and bewildered. Where had the man come *from?* And where had he *gone?* Felix thought this was the most wonderful thing he had ever seen. However, a still greater wonder was to come.

The dog picked up the wand in her mouth again. She waved it by jerking her head up and down. Then another man slowly rose from the empty box. He was completely different from the man in the top hat. He was a Chinese in a long yellow gown. His head was shaved except for a long plaited queue of hair that hung down his back.

The Chinese man stepped from the box and bowed to the dog. The dog tucked her head to bow back. The man then walked to the edge of the stage. He bowed to the audience. Then he stepped back several feet.

He never said a word, but raised his hands above his head, with the palms turned toward the audience. They were empty. Then he brought his hands down and rubbed his palms together. Felix watched, spellbound, as a large square of bright red silk slowly worked its way from between his empty hands. It fell to the stage.

The Chinese man got down on his knees and smoothed the silk out on the stage. Then he raised one corner and peeked under it. He did not like what he saw. He dropped the corner, then used his other hand to raise the opposite corner on the side away from the audience.

This time he nodded, pleased with what he saw. He brought his other hand around, grasping the two corners of the red cloth on the side away from the audience, and jerked the silk away with a quick wave of his hands.

A large glass bowl of water now sat on the stage! Two red apples bobbed in the water. Where had it come from? The cloth had been *flat* on the stage before the magician lifted it up. In some manner he must have shoved the bowl forward from under his gown when he lifted the cloth.

But that seemed impossible too. The bowl was brimful. How could the magician have moved it without spilling water to give his trick away? How could he have walked with a full bowl of water under his gown? It seemed to Felix that this was indeed *real* magic!

There were still more surprises to come. The Chinese magician went back to the box. He stepped inside it, after bowing to the dog. Felix expected the man to disappear as the first one had. Instead, the audience got an even bigger surprise.

The Chinese magician raised his hand to his head. He hesitated. He seemed unsure of himself, as if he did not know what to do next. Then, with a quick jerk of his hand, *he pulled off the top of his head!*

Felix felt as if someone had hit him! He thought he had been surprised before, but this surpassed anything he had ever seen in his life.

The magician's bald head with the queue attached was only a skullcap that the man had worn over his real head. Now he had pulled it off. He opened his squinted eyes. His lips moved to change the shape of his mouth. Then he took a pair of rimless glasses from a pocket under the gown. When he put them on, the audience saw the face of the man in the top hat!

Smiling, this amazing man dropped out of sight into the box. It seemed to Felix that he was gone only a second. Then he rose again, wearing the dress suit in which he had first appeared. He stepped out of the box and, with the dog beside him, said in a deep, rich voice, "Good evening, ladies and gentlemen. I am The Great Lafayette!"

He half turned and motioned toward the dog. She sat up on her hind legs and tucked her head in a cute bow.

"And this," he said, his voice full of pride, "is my friend, my partner, and my fellow magician—Beauty!"

The audience broke into loud applause. None among them clapped harder than Felix Marshal. He said he beat his hands together until his palms were sore.

Lafayette was a quick-change artist as well as a magician. He could step behind a screen for just a few seconds and come back as an entirely different person. This was done by wearing special clothing he could slip in and out of almost instantly. Mustaches, wigs, and the way he twisted his face aided the effect. This ability to be several people added to the interest of his act.

Beauty had a part in several of Lafayette's turns. Felix could not remember them all. One he did recall was where Lafayette made Beauty vanish and reappear several times. In the end Beauty made Lafayette disappear.

The trick began with Lafayette's rolling a large box on stage. The box was raised high enough from the floor that the audience could see under it. There was no way anyone hidden inside could slip out through the bottom without being seen.

"Lafayette turned the box around so we could see all four sides," Felix told me. "The back and sides were solid—or looked that way. The front of the box was a door that could be lifted up. Lafayette opened the door to show us that the box was empty.

"The magician turned to the dog and said, 'Where's Bobby?'

"Beauty trotted off to the wings and returned with a stuffed bear in her mouth. Lafayette took the toy and thanked Beauty for her trouble.

" 'This is a very unusual trick,' Lafayette told us. 'The trick was taught to me by a fakir in Ceylon after I saved his life from an angry mob. Now watch very closely as I place this stuffed animal in the box.'

"But before he could place the toy in the box, Beauty jumped in and stretched out. Lafayette pretended to be very angry.

" 'Get out of there!' he yelled at her.

"Beauty shook her head from side to side. The audience laughed, and I laughed louder than anyone. Again Lafayette ordered the dog to get out of the box. Again she shook her head to say No.

" 'Then I'll show you!' Lafayette cried.

"He went over and picked up the magic wand from the floor where the dog had dropped it.

" 'This is your last chance,' he told Beauty. 'Come out of that box—or else!'

"Beauty shook her head again. Lafayette closed the door, shutting her in the box. He waved his wand in the air and said some strange words. Then he reopened the box. The dog had vanished! The audience applauded loudly. But I didn't. I liked the dog. I did *not* want to see her go away.

" 'Now,' he said, closing the door of the box, 'I will go back to my famous toy-bear trick. Please watch very closely, for this trick has mystified kings and queens!'

"He opened the box door. Beauty was back inside! Lafayette looked astonished. 'How did you get back in there?' he asked. His voice was loud with anger.

"I was so surprised that I jumped up and cried, 'How did they do that?' Mother roughly pulled me back in my seat. She said that if I embarrassed her again she would take me home. It wasn't my fault. How could anyone keep still at a wonderful show like this?

"Lafayette slammed the door shut. He really seemed angry now. He opened it. Beauty had vanished again. He closed the door and reopened it. She was back again. He opened and closed the door several times more, working very fast. Beauty continued to appear and disappear.

"The last time she reappeared, Lafayette threw his hands in the air. 'I give up!' he cried. 'Stay in there if you wish!'

"But Beauty did not want to tease him any longer. She jumped out of the box. Lafayette got in himself and pulled the door shut. Beauty sniffed at the box. She barked. We heard Lafayette's voice from inside telling her to go away. The dog barked again, and a man came from the wings. He knocked on the door of the box and asked Lafayette if he was inside.

" 'Of course I am!' we heard Lafayette yell.

"But when the stagehand opened the box within a second after Lafayette called out that he was inside, there was nobody there! The stagehand rolled the box around, so we could see that the magician had neither slipped out nor was hiding behind the box. Then Beauty jumped up on top of the box and rode it offstage as the stagehand pushed the box toward the wings. The curtain closed. Then Lafayette and Beauty came back to take their bows."

The memory of this show stayed with Felix Marshal for the rest of his life. However, historians of magic do not rate The Great Lafayette as great as his name. They say he was a great showman—none better—but he was not an inventor of tricks. He could take tricks developed by others and dress them up. He made his reputation by combining quick-change routines and magic.

His lack of originality was the reason that Lafayette was not doing well until he teamed with Beauty, the magic dog. She helped him become the highest-paid conjurer of his time.

Lafayette and Beauty were just starting their climb to fame when Felix Marshal saw them. Their partnership would go on for another twelve years. Then Beauty died of old age, and Lafayette died just five days later. He had always said that he would not live long if he lost Beauty.

Before he had Beauty, Lafayette never wanted a dog. In fact, when she was thrust on him, he was angry.

It all came about as a joke. Harry Houdini, one of the great magicians of all time, thought it up. It annoyed Lafayette at first, but later he said that it was the most fortunate and wonderful thing that ever happened to him.

3 * A Present from Houdini

THE GREAT LAFAYETTE was originally called Sigmund Neuberger. Sigmund was born in 1872 in Munich, Germany. His father was a jeweler who expected his son to follow the family business.

Young Sigmund had other ideas. As a child he was shy and lonely. No one paid any attention to him. He wanted attention very badly, but did not know how to attract it. Somehow he got the idea that becoming a stage performer would make him an important person.

He had no idea how to go about becoming an actor. Then in 1885 he saw a performer who claimed to be an American Indian. This man (who was actually a Frenchman) billed himself as the "Indian William Tell." He did fancy shooting with a bow and arrow. Young Sigmund was greatly impressed. He decided to build an act of his own, patterning it after what he had seen.

Sigmund knew better than to ask his father for money to buy props for a stage act. Sam Neuberger had no use for actors. So the young man tried a sly trick. He found that doctors sometimes prescribed archery for patients who needed to build their chest, shoulders, and arm muscles.

Sigmund mentioned this to his father. Sam Neuberger was delighted. His son was still scrawny, and he thought the exercise might help make a man of the boy. He bought a complete archery set for his son.

Sigmund worked hard and developed into a very good archer. He could shoot an arrow to the center of the target and then split this arrow with another shot right after it.

Then in 1889, Samuel Neuberger took his seventeen-year-old son with him on a business trip to New York. He was trying to teach the boy to be a wholesale jeweler. But he was wasting his time. As soon as Sigmund had a chance, he visited a vaudeville booking agency and talked the agent into finding him a spot with his archery act. That night when Sam Neuberger returned to his hotel, he found a note from his son.

"I have decided to do both you and the jewelry business a favor," Sigmund wrote. "I shall find a different profession. I have become a stage performer in American vaudeville. When I am famous, I am sure you will forgive me and be very proud of your son."

Neuberger was enraged. He rushed to the police, but they refused to hunt for the missing boy. Sigmund had joined a traveling troupe that played small towns along the Atlantic coast.

His archery act was not dramatic enough to attract

attention, and he was soon dropped from the show. Going back to New York, he worked digging ditches for a sewer line until a man he met got him a job as a stagehand at a small theater. While working here, Sigmund saw several magicians. He decided to become one himself.

Sigmund tried to learn magic by watching the magicians both backstage and onstage. This caused him to neglect his own work. He was fired.

His next job was as a dressing assistant to a quick-change artist. This performer billed himself as "The Man Who Is Many Men." He had twenty different costumes, which he changed with bewildering speed. The costumes were all split down the back, legs and arms, but were held together with thin steel-band springs hidden inside the garments.

In the act, the performer would appear onstage in a drum major's costume. Then he would step quickly behind a screen. He would grasp the front of the costume and jerk it off with one pull. Sigmund would be waiting behind the screen with the next costume, holding it open so that the Man Who Is Many Men could slip into it instantly. When Sigmund let go of the garment, the springs pulled the costume around the performer. He would then slap on a fake mustache or a new wig before stepping back on stage as a different character. It was all done so fast that it appeared to the audience as magic.

Sigmund learned enough as assistant to the quick-change artist to work up an act of his own. He was not very good in the beginning and had to work in smaller theaters as he gained experience. He got better as time passed, but was never able to get bookings into the big theaters.

This went on for years. Sigmund grew increasingly bitter. He convinced himself that he did not have a friend in the world. Offstage, he would not talk with his fellow actors. He thought they were trying to steal the secrets of the magic tricks he had worked into his act.

Sigmund finally got a break in 1898. He was now back in New York, where he had left his father almost ten years ago. Everywhere he went he heard people talking about the wonderful magician who had come from China with marvelous new tricks.

Neuberger was out of a job. He spent each day tramping from one booking office to another. Then one afternoon he passed the theater where the Chinese magician was appearing. There was a large poster in front of the lobby. It showed a tall, bald Chinese man dressed in a long gown. He was billed as "Ching Ling Foo, Celestial Wizard from the Imperial Court of China."

Sigmund was suddenly struck with an exciting idea. One of the secrets of a quick-change artist is to wear several costumes at the same time, so that he only has to jerk the top one off to expose the one underneath. Then he does not have to take an extra second to slip into a new costume, which makes the change faster.

The long Chinese gown that Ching Ling Foo wore would be ideal to conceal the drum-major uniform that was part of Neuberger's act. Also, Sigmund had never played a Chinese role. He liked the idea of trying.

He bought a ticket to the show and watched Ching Ling Foo's performance. It was a remarkably good act. Sigmund went again the next day. The first time he had gone to *see* the performance. The second time he went to study it.

All the characters he used in his quick-change act were drawn from life. Once he walked for two hours, following a Scotsman in kilts who was visiting New York. He closely watched every move the man made, filing each detail in his mind to use later when he acted the part of a Scotsman. In the same manner, he watched Irish policemen, Italian fruit dealers, English gentlemen, and drunken bums. Thus his performances were true to life.

Now he was studying Ching Ling Foo in the same way. He noted the way the Chinese magician nodded his head, raised his arms, and how he walked and smiled. Then back in his hotel room, Sigmund practiced in front of a mirror until he almost *was* Ching Ling Foo.

He had a Chinese gown made. Then he got a skullcap with a long queue attached. When he put the gown and cap on and used some makeup around his eyes, he looked surprisingly like the Chinese magician.

There were only two performers with whom Neuberger was friendly. One was Erich Weiss, who called himself Harry Houdini, after the French magician Jean Robert-Houdin. The other was W. E. Robinson. Houdini later became one of the most famous magicians of all time. Robinson had been a trick maker for Alexander Herrmann, another of the truly great magicians. Neuberger showed his Chinese makeup to Houdini. His fellow magician was delighted.

"How are you going to use the character?" Houdini asked.

"As an extra character in my changes."

"No," Houdini objected. "This is too good for that. Ching Ling Foo is going on a tour when his New York engagement closes. Then he leaves for England. What you should do is to work up a complete imitation of the Chinese magician. It will go over big."

"But I'd have to do his tricks," Sigmund protested. "I couldn't do that."

"Why not?" Houdini insisted. "In a short vaudeville act you would only have to do three or four. Actually, his best trick—producing that bowl of water from nowhere —is a very old stunt."

"I've never seen it before," Neuberger said.

"The trick is so old it seems new," Houdini said. "They have been doing the trick in China for over two hundred years. A Chinese magician brought it to France in 1842. He used a small bowl. Then Robert-Houdin invented a special quick-release cover so he could use larger bowls."

"I don't understand why such a wonderful trick was forgotten," Sigmund said.

"Too many magicians caught on," Houdini explained. "Audiences got tired of seeing so much of the same thing. The trick was dropped and forgotten."

"He certainly had the bowl under his gown, but how

did he keep the water from spilling out when he walked?"

"A waterproof cap fits over the bowl," Houdini explained. "This prevents the water from spilling when the bowl is hung sideways on a hook under the magician's clothes. It is unhooked and slid under the cloth when the magician raises a corner. The hard part of the trick is to get the waterproof cap off the bowl without the audience seeing it.

"Robert-Houdin tightened the cap on the bowl with a special ratchet catch. This had a spring that would release the cover with a touch of the magician's thumb. He would catch the loose cover with two fingers and keep it hidden under the cloth as he drew it away. The audience never sees the hidden cover.

"Robert-Houdin hid the covered bowl under the tails of his dress suit. Ching Ling Foo probably has it under his gown. There's a slit in the gown we can't see. Then, when he raises up a corner of the silk, it makes a screen so he can shove the bowl into place without being seen."

"I can do that," Sigmund said. "It is basically a very simple trick."

"Aren't most magic tricks simple?" Houdini asked.

"Once they are explained, yes," his fellow magician said. "But it takes genius to figure them out in the first place."

Sigmund Neuberger took Houdini's advice. He worked out an impersonation of Ching Ling Foo, which he did as part of his quick-change act. He came out first as himself. Then he ducked behind a screen. He slipped the Chinese gown over his dress suit, pulled on the skull-cap with the queue, and stepped back out.

At first he tried to use makeup to give himself Oriental eyes. This took too long. He kept experimenting and found that if he just narrowed his eyes and *acted* like a Chinese, he could pass without eye makeup.

He auditioned the impersonation part of the act for the Keith-Albee vaudeville booking agent. Keith-Albee was the largest theater chain of the time. The agent liked the act. He gave Neuberger a tryout in a local theater. The act was a hit, and Neuberger was signed to a year's contract.

However, the agent did not think Neuberger was a grand enough name for a magician. After a lot of thought, Sigmund picked The Great Lafayette as his stage name. He took the name from a statue of Lafayette, the revolutionary war hero, that he had seen in a park. The agent liked the name, and Sigmund used it for the rest of his life.

As The Great Lafayette, Sigmund was a vaudeville hit for two seasons. Then the novelty of the Chinese imper-sonation began to wear off. Sigmund knew that he had to come up with some new idea or he would be back where he started.

Once again his friend Houdini came to his rescue—but Houdini didn't know he was helping The Great La-fayette stay in business. He thought he was playing a joke on his friend.

Houdini's act, billed as "The King of Cards," had failed. He tried a straight magic act. It also failed. Next he tried to make a comeback as The Escape King. In this act he permitted men from the audience to tie him up in ropes, chains, handcuffs, and even straitjackets. He would escape from them without difficulty. No lock, rope, or chain could hold him. He was doing better with this act. Eventually it would make him world famous.

But at this time, he was just getting started. He was booked on a vaudeville circuit that brought him and The Great Lafayette to the same town, but to different theaters.

The two men met in the lobby of a theatrical rooming house. Lafayette, as we shall call him from this time on, was angry and bitter. His assistant had stolen some of his costumes and left to start his own act. Then Lafayette had quarreled with the stage manager over the lighting of his act. To cap his troubles, he had just received a letter from the booking agent. It said that The Great Lafayette act would not be rebooked next season.

Lafayette complained to Houdini that the world was against him.

"I haven't got a friend in the world!" he said bitterly.

"What about me?" Houdini asked.

"I guess you and Robinson are as near to friends as anyone," Lafayette replied. "But Robinson is in France, and I only see you once a year."

They talked for a while about W. E. Robinson. He had also worked out a Chinese magician act. Unlike Lafayette, who put on an imitation of Ching Ling Foo, Robinson billed himself as "Chung Lung Soo" and claimed to be a real Chinese.

"I hear that Robinson is doing a bullet-catching act," Lafayette told Houdini. "He has a firing squad of six men come on stage and shoot at him. He catches the six bullets on a plate held in front of his heart."

"I hope you aren't thinking of trying that trick," Houdini said, showing alarm. "Several magicians have been killed doing it."

"I need something big," Lafayette replied. "I'm being dropped next season."

"Well, think of something less dangerous," Houdini replied. "I won't do that trick myself. Robinson will get himself killed if he keeps that trick."

As it happened, Houdini was right. Chung Lung Soo was killed sometime later when something went wrong with the trick guns used in the dangerous act.

Lafayette was so unhappy that Houdini thought a joke might cheer him up. The next afternoon, just before Lafayette's matinee performance, Houdini stopped at his friend's theater. He carried a small dog in his arms. Houdini never told where he got the dog. Some say he found it in an alley.

Houdini went to Lafayette's dressing room. He shoved the dog into the surprised magician's arms.

"You said you haven't a friend in the world," Houdini told Lafayette. "That is terrible. So I brought you this dog."

"But—!" Lafayette began.

"They say a dog is man's best friend, don't they?"

"But—!"

"Now you not only have a friend, you have a *best* friend!"

"Harry, you are crazy!" Lafayette cried. "I don't—"

"Please! Don't try to thank me. I know I'm crazy for parting with such a wonderful friend, but you need her more than I," Houdini went on, not letting Lafayette say anything.

With the excuse that he had to get to his own theater, Houdini rushed out. Lafayette stood with the dog in his arms, looking bewildered.

The dog looked up at him, and some of his anger left Lafayette. He noticed that the dog had very beautiful brown eyes. She licked his hand.

Lafayette smiled. "You must be hungry," he said. "You are trying to eat me!"

The call boy knocked on the dressing room door to alert Lafayette that he was next on the bill. The magician put the dog on the chair in front of his dressing table.

"Stay there until I come back," he said. "Then I'll take you back to that crazy Houdini. A dog is the last thing I need."

The dog could not understand his words, of course. But the tone of Lafayette's voice let her know that he was displeased. She dropped her head and looked sad.

Lafayette checked his costume to make sure the second one he wore under the first did not show. He also checked the "loads"—objects in his pockets which he would magically produce later—to make sure they were in place.

Then, ready to go onstage, he paused at the dressing-room door to look back at the dog. She had her front paws on the table and was sniffing at her image in the mirror.

Lafayette smiled.

"She *is* a beautiful creature," he said.

4 * Beauty Becomes a Magician

THE GREAT LAFAYETTE'S act at this time was a mixture of quick-change characters and magic tricks. He opened with his impersonation of Ching Ling Foo, but did not use the water-bowl trick until later.

He opened by seeming to pull Chinese fortune cookies out of the air. Actually, they were in pockets hidden in the folds of his long Oriental gown. As he mysteriously pulled one cookie from the air, his other hand—unseen by the audience—took another cookie from its hiding place. The cookie was palmed. That is, he held it in the palm of his open hand by slightly curving his fingers. When he raised his hand, palm turned away from the audience, his hand looked empty. Then with a twist of his fingers, he would push the cookie up. It looked as if he had snatched it from the air.

With the audience's attention on this hand and its magic cookie, his other hand was palming another cookie to repeat the trick. He kept this up until twenty cookies had been produced and given to people in the audience. Next Lafayette—still in Oriental dress—showed his empty hands to the audience. As he turned to show first one side of the audience his hands and then the other, one hand—unseen by those watching—deftly took an egg from the loading pocket. This he palmed. Then he raised his hand to his mouth and seemed to pull the egg from his mouth.

The audience applauded, but Lafayette did not wait for them to stop. His act moved rapidly. One trick followed another so fast that the audience never had time to think about how the tricks were done.

Lafayette had a large platter with a dome cover sitting on a magician's table. After taking the egg from his mouth, he removed the cover from this platter. The platter was large—the size a cook would use for a Thanksgiving turkey. He set the cover down beside the platter.

He then took the egg and cracked it. A newborn chick dropped out on the platter. The chick was a toy, made of cotton and feathers. But Lafayette moved so fast that the audience did not know this. He picked up the cover and put it back over the platter to hide the chick.

At the same time, Lafayette cried loudly, "Behold!"

He quickly raised the platter cover again. A frightened, full-grown chicken jumped off the platter. Beating its wings and squawking, the chicken fled across the stage. The audience roared with laughter.

Like all effective magic tricks, this one was simple to

do. The platter cover was actually a small cage. The bottom, which the audience could not see, was locked in place. There was a small spring in the handle on top of the cover. When this was pressed by the magician's fingers, it released the bottom of the cage from the cover. The chicken was loaded into the cage before the act. It was dark in the cage and the chicken remained quiet. To do the trick, Lafayette placed the cotton chick on the platter. The chick was mashed flat by the bottom of the cage when the magician replaced the cover.

The bottom of the cage was the same shape as the platter and fitted inside the platter. It would not be seen when Lafayette released the catch. Then when he raised the top, the chicken would be uncovered. To the audience it looked like real magic. Lafayette had changed a newborn chick into a full-grown chicken. The chicken, which had been quiet because of the darkness in the cage, was frightened by the light and applause. It beat its wings, jumped to the stage, and fled to give a comic ending to the trick.

In the split second that the audience's attention followed the escaping chicken, Lafayette stepped through a slit in the curtain backdrop. He jerked loose two fasteners on the shoulders of his Chinese gown. It dropped to the floor. He was wearing a drum major's uniform under the gown. He stooped and placed the drum major's hat right at the edge of the curtain. Later he would make the hat seem to appear by magic.

He then stepped back through the curtain, after

removing his skullcap with the queue he used for the Chinese part of the act.

This all happened so fast that when the audience looked back at the magician it seemed that he had magically changed into a different person.

The act called for Lafayette to produce a baton magically from the air. He would wave the baton to accompany himself as he marched in place, whistling a patriotic tune. He would then toss the baton in the air several times and make it vanish in midair. Finally, he would produce the hat, then pull a large American flag on a five-foot pole from the hat. This he would wave for a patriotic finale.

Things went well until he began tossing the baton in the air. Just before he made it vanish in midair, the audience started to laugh.

A chill went through the alarmed magician. He loved to make his audience laugh. But he wanted the laughs to be in the right places, such as when the frightened chicken fled across the stage. When an audience laughs unexpectedly, it means that something has gone wrong.

Lafayette started to sweat. He had no idea what had gone wrong. He continued and made the baton vanish. The audience kept laughing. He looked around. He saw the dog he had left in his dressing room. She had nosed open the dressing room door and had followed him on stage. She trotted over, sat up on her haunches, and barked at the flustered magician. The audience laughed louder.

For a breathless moment Lafayette was stunned. However, one of the first things a beginning performer learns is to think fast when something goes wrong on stage. A basic rule of showmanship is to try to work the mistake into the act. Then the audience will never realize that there has been trouble.

"What can I do to bring the dog into the act?" Lafayette thought desperately.

Ten years' experience and a thousand previous mistakes had taught him to think rapidly. He stooped and picked up the dog.

"What is the trouble?" he asked her.

At the same time, he pulled the dog around so that her muzzle came up to his ear as he cocked his head toward her. He opened his mouth in surprise as if she had whispered something in his ear.

He put his free hand to his head, discovering that he did not have his hat on.

"Thanks for telling me!" he said in a loud stage whisper that the audience could hear. Then to the audience, he added, "Excuse me for a moment."

He put down the dog and stepped through the opening in the stage backdrop, put the hat on his head, and came back. He resumed the act, finishing with the production of the flag from the hat.

The flag was made of sheer silk and took up little space when tightly folded. The flagpole was jointed and collapsed into a small space. When the pole was extended and the flag unfurled, they looked very large.

Lafayette picked the dog up again when he finished his turn. He bowed and received the loudest applause he had ever gotten on stage.

At that moment, Sigmund Neuberger was happier than he had ever been before in his life. This was the way he had dreamed of being received by an audience.

He took the dog back to his dressing room. In his joy, he hugged her tightly and put her down on the dressing-table top.

"You were wonderful!" he cried. "You behaved just like a seasoned trouper. From now on, you and I are partners. Come, let us shake hands on the deal!"

He put his hand out. But the only trick the dog knew was to sit up and beg. However, she was very intelligent. Alley dogs, who have to survive on their own, often are. They have to be smart to keep alive. Lafayette quickly taught her to shake hands. He began by raising her paw and putting it in his palm. He kept repeating this, patting her head, and praising her each time he did. She quickly learned that she was considered a "nice doggie" indeed if she placed her paw in an outstretched hand.

Lafayette was delighted at how quickly the dog learned. He patted her head again. She licked his hand and wagged her tail so hard that she knocked a jar of cold cream off the dressing table. It hit the floor and broke.

Lafayette just laughed. He got down and cleaned up the mess, saving enough of the cream to remove his greasepaint makeup.

He looked fondly at the dog. "You must have a

name," he told her. "What shall we call you? You are beautiful. So let's call you Beauty. How do you like that?"

Lafayette always insisted that Beauty was the most beautiful dog that ever lived. Actually, her looks were quite ordinary, but the magician became very angry if anyone told him so. However, all who knew her said that she was an uncommonly smart dog.

Ideas in which he could use the dog in his different acts tumbled through the magician's head. He sat down at the table and started spreading cold cream on his face to remove the greasepaint. He kept talking to the dog. It never occurred to him that such a smart dog could not understand every word he said. For the rest of his life, Lafayette appeared to think that Beauty was human in every way except her shape.

He was still talking happily and wiping his face with a towel when the door opened with an angry bang.

Lafayette looked around. Two enraged teenage sisters were at the door. They were a song-and-dance team that followed the magician on the vaudeville bill. Beauty's interruption and the way Lafayette worked her into the act had caused his turn to run long. This had shortened the time for the girls' act. They were yelling and threatening the magician.

Before Lafayette could reply, Beauty started barking at the girls. Still yelling, they retreated to the door.

"You don't need to fear Beauty," Lafayette told them. "She will not bite you, but if you don't get out of here, *I* will!"

At this point the girls' father, who was also their manager, came running in. He was ready to punch Lafayette in the nose. Fortunately, the stage manager and theater owner came and broke up the fight.

Lafayette was told to stick to his allotted time or his contract would be broken. The others left, and he went back to removing his makeup. He thought no more of the fight or the threat to end his contract. The backstage world of vaudeville was filled with temperamental, jealous performers. There were arguments and fights all the time. It was all part of show business.

Lafayette kept up his conversation with the dog as he changed from his costume to street clothes. The more he talked, the more possibilities he saw in having Beauty in the act. He was certain that the new act he envisioned would be popular enough to cause the Keith-Albee booking agent to renew Lafayette's contract for the next year.

The applause he and Beauty got was proof to him that they would make a very popular team.

"It has taken me ten years," he told the dog, "but at last my troubles are over! We'll go on together to fame and fortune!"

The Great Lafayette was right about their going on to fame and fortune. But he was wrong about their troubles' being over. He was to have troubles for the rest of his life.

In fact, trouble was waiting for him back at the theatrical rooming house where he was staying. Mrs. O'Brien —history does not tell us the lady's first name—was the

landlady. She did not allow pets in her house. So when
The Great Lafayette came in that night with a dog, the
stage was set for a battle between an angry magician and
an angrier landlady.

5 * Beauty and the Beast

LANDLADIES WHO RAN theatrical boardinghouses in the 1890's had to be tough. Vaudeville did not pay well. The people in it were always short of money. While many vaudevillians were honest, many others were not. They made a fine art of sneaking out without paying their bills.

Even the honest ones were troublesome. Cooking in rooms was forbidden because of fire laws. But many a poor actor removed the mantle from his room's gas light and used the small flame to fry food. This was very dangerous.

Sometimes one actor would rent a room as a single. Then he would try to sneak in several of his friends to sleep without paying.

Actors were always up to something. A rooming-house manager had to be constantly on guard to keep from being cheated. Mrs. O'Brien was well fitted for this job.

She was almost as broad as she was tall. Her face looked like red brick. She trusted no one and was strong enough to throw out any actor who disagreed with her rules.

Her roomers called her The Beast. They complained, cursed, and swore they would never put up at her place again. But her house was clean and cheap, and her cooking was superb. So even the loudest complainers came back the next time they were in town.

For her part, Mrs. O'Brien honestly thought all performers were thieves. Next to actors, she disliked animals. She would not permit one in the house. Lafayette knew this. So he cautiously opened the front door and peered in before entering with Beauty.

The front parlor was empty, and Mrs. O'Brien's door was closed. She had a room next to the parlor at the foot of the stairs.

Lafayette picked up the dog and went inside. He closed the door softly and hurried past Mrs. O'Brien's room. He thought he had succeeded in sneaking the dog past her. Unfortunately for him, the landlady had very sharp ears. Lafayette and Beauty had just reached the stairs when Mrs. O'Brien came out of her room.

"What is *this?*" she cried, her fat face flushing with anger.

"It is nothing to get disturbed about," Lafayette said hastily. "I am just—"

"I know what you are doing!" the angry woman cried. "Don't try to tell me some outrageous lie! Get that miserable, flea-bitten animal out of here!"

"Madame!" Lafayette said, his rage equalling her own. "This is not a miserable, flea-bitten animal! Beauty is no ordinary dog."

"Don't try to blarney me!" she retorted. "I know an alley mutt when I see one!"

"Beauty is not an alley dog! Her pedigree goes back to royal hounds kept by the kings of France in the seventeenth century. You should be proud to have such a fine animal in your house."

"Sure, and if the mutt be the pet poodle of the blessed Saint Patrick himself, the thing does *not* come in *my* house!"

Lafayette tried to argue. The enraged landlady threatened to throw both Lafayette and the dog in the street if he didn't take Beauty away.

Lafayette knew that she could and would do it, too. Once two wrestlers had argued with her over house rules. She knocked one out with a chair and broke a ceramic water pitcher over the head of the other. Then, grabbing the collars of the two unconscious men, she dragged them to the door and pitched them down the steps into the street.

Lafayette retreated before her wrath. He left the house with Beauty and sat down on the steps to decide what to do next. He had no place to sleep. He would not be paid until the end of the week and had no money to rent another room. Even if he could have found another place to stay, he doubted that any of them would permit him to bring the dog to his room.

Lafayette never forgot this experience. In later years he often told people about the "cruelty" of Mrs. O'Brien in refusing to let him take Beauty to his room. Many thought him odd because of the way he refused to be parted from the dog. Actually this was rooted in his loveless life. He had never been close to his father and brother. Then, when he went into show business, he continued to be lonely. He had no really close friends. Robinson and Houdini were the only ones who came close to being friends, and he seldom saw them. Beauty was the first thing that he had ever really loved in his life, and she seems to have been the last thing he loved too. All his life Lafayette was a very bitter man.

Years later, when he was rich and famous, he put a sign over the door of his home in London. It said, "The more I see of people, the more I love my dog!"

Finally, Lafayette went to the apartment house next door to Mrs. O'Brien's rooming house. He awoke the custodian, bribing the man with a fifty-cent piece to let him and the dog sleep in the basement that night.

Lafayette awoke sore and stiff the next morning, for his bed had been a pile of rags on the floor. However, he did not regret it. He had to leave the dog in the basement for a short time while he went back to Mrs. O'Brien's house. He had to shave and clean up and get clean clothes to wear to the theater. Also, he had to eat. Mrs. O'Brien furnished meals for her roomers.

Lafayette had never cared for an animal before. He never thought about feeding and providing water for the dog he left in the basement. Beauty, as an experienced alley dog, knew how to take care of herself. She crawled out the basement window and went in search of food among the garbage cans.

The magician was frantic when he came back and found her gone. He almost got in a fight with the janitor, whom he blamed for letting the dog get away.

He started searching the alleys and streets. He stopped everyone he passed, asking if he or she had seen a "beautiful dog." No one had. It is more than possible that some of them had seen the dog, but that when Lafayette inquired about a "beautiful dog," they had visions of something like a Russian wolfhound, a collie, or the like.

Lafayette hunted for over an hour. He was in despair. He had convinced himself that some thief had stolen the dog because she was so beautiful.

He was about ready to give up. Then, as a last hope, he stopped and asked a policeman on a corner if he had seen a lost beautiful dog.

"No," the policeman said. "Not a beautiful dog. But when you were coming down the street I noticed this mutt was following you."

Lafayette turned quickly. His face lighted with joy. Beauty was standing there about ten feet back, looking at him. She had picked him up sometime before. However, his frantic, angry manner made her afraid to approach him. She had trotted along behind him for at least half an hour. He, intent on his search, never thought of looking back. Those he asked never dreamed that the "beautiful dog" he sought was the little part-hound.

The magician scooped the dog up in his arms. He was

almost in tears. The policeman smiled and shook his head. In years to come a lot of other people would also smile and shake their heads over Lafayette's unusual love for his dog. All agreed that the magician was a very intelligent man, an extremely good businessman, and a great showman, but where the dog was concerned, they said he was just plain crazy.

After his first smile, the policeman frowned and became businesslike. "Sure, and we have a leash law in this town," he told Lafayette. "If you let your dog run loose, the dogcatcher is going to pick her up."

"I'll be careful," Lafayette promised. "And please don't call Beauty my dog. She isn't. We're partners."

"Partners?" the policeman repeated, wondering if he should take this lunatic to the police station.

"Oh, yes. I am The Great Lafayette, and this is my partner Beauty. We are performing this week at the Keith theater in a mystifying act of incredible wonders."

"Oh," said the policeman, looking relieved. "It is an actor you be. That explains your odd behavior."

Lafayette did not think his behavior was odd at all, but he was grateful to the policeman for helping him find Beauty. He took the dog to the theater, leaving her with the doorman. Then he got two tickets to the evening show. He took them back to give to the policeman, but he had been relieved by another. So Lafayette gave the tickets to two ragged boys he saw digging in some trash boxes to see what they could find.

"In the fourth act of the show," Lafayette told the

boys, "you will see the most wonderful magician who ever lived, and the most beautiful dog. When they finish their act, I want you to yell loud enough to raise the roof off the theater. Then after you leave the show, you tell everyone what a wonderful act these two partners have. That is the way you pay for these tickets. Is it a deal?"

It was.

Lafayette hurried back to the theater. He wanted to make the mistakes and accident of the previous night's show a part of the act. He spent the better part of two hours teaching Beauty her role in the show. He had only one difficulty. She did not want to wait in the wings until her time came to trot out on the stage. She wanted to be with Lafayette all the time. He solved this problem by putting the dog on a leash held by a stagehand. When Lafayette gave the cue, the dog was released and came on to do her part.

The audience that night was as enthusiastic as the previous one had been. Lafayette was delighted. He sent a telegram to the Keith-Albee booking agent in New York, telling the agent how well the new act was doing.

Two days later Lafayette ended his run and moved to the next town on the circuit. As usual when his spirits were high, something happened to put him a bad mood again. This time it was the train conductor, who refused to let Lafayette take Beauty into the passenger coach.

The angry magician argued so long and so loudly that the conductor signaled the engineer to start the train. It pulled out without Lafayette. The magician had to take a later train and put Beauty in the baggage car. They barely arrived in time to rush to the theater and go into their act.

The theater manager was angry at Lafayette. He thought right up to show time that they would have to put on the bill without the magician. The advertisements said that there would be a conjuring act. If none appeared, any ticket buyer could get his or her money back.

Lafayette and Beauty were such a hit that the theater manager forgot his anger. He was beaming when the magician and his dog finished their act.

More importantly, the manager showed his appreciation in a way that delighted Lafayette. First, he sent a telegram to the booking agency in New York. He praised the act highly.

IT IS THE BEST THING YOU HAVE SENT ME IN FIVE YEARS, the telegram said. THE DOG WAS WONDERFUL. THE MAGICIAN WITH HER WAS GOOD TOO.

Lafayette was not angry at being put second to Beauty in the telegram. He was delighted. He was even more happy at the second kindness the manager showed him.

The magician had told him that they were late because of the trouble of getting Beauty on the train. The manager happened to know the local agent for the railway company. He talked to the agent.

"We can't have a dog in the passenger car," the agent said. "However, if the dog is as great as you say, she should get some consideration. Let me work on it."

Then the manager talked to another friend, who operated a hotel in the town. He put on a real act of his own as he explained how Lafayette had to guard this wonderful dog every second to keep it from being stolen.

The hotel keeper agreed to let Lafayette keep Beauty in his room. However, he did not want other patrons to know it. Some would surely object to having a dog in the house. Others might want to bring in their own pets.

"So if he will bring the dog in through the employees' entrance in the back, I will let Mr. Lafayette keep her in his room," the hotel keeper said. "Also, he must prevent her from barking."

This worked well. The dog was so well behaved that the hotel keeper telephoned the manager of a hotel in the next town on Lafayette's tour. He made similar arrangements for the dog to stay there with the magician.

When the act closed and moved on to the next town, the railroad agent arranged for Lafayette to have one of the compartments on the train. This was a small private room at the end of the coach. Here he could keep Beauty with him without the passengers' in the coach seeing the dog.

Two weeks and two towns later, Lafayette found that the theater manager's kindness had brought the magician and Beauty another stroke of good luck. The glowing telegram praising the "dog magician" aroused the booking agency's interest. He had never heard of anything like this.

The agent waited a week and then put in a telephone call to the manager of the next theater where Lafayette and Beauty appeared. He got another good report about the Magic Dog. The two reports caused the agency to send a scout to check on the show.

Jacob Levy, the scout, was very good at spotting talent. He did not let Lafayette know that he was scouting the show. He took a seat in the audience. He watched the show carefully. The next day he returned. He did not watch Lafayette. He watched the audience, checking its reaction to the show.

On the third day, Levy came to the theater before the show. He went to Lafayette's dressing room. He introduced himself. Then Lafayette introduced the talent scout to Beauty.

"Shake hands with Mr. Levy," Lafayette told her.

Beauty raised her paw. Levy was delighted. He actually smiled at the dog. This was unusual for him. Those who knew him said that Levy should have been an undertaker. He always looked gloomy.

"If you keep this dog in the act," he told Lafayette, "Keith-Albee will surely sign you for next year. However, it is not a good act."

Lafayette was outraged. "What do you mean, not a good act?" he cried. "What do you think all that applause was for? They loved Beauty and me!"

By this time Lafayette had trained Beauty in the opening turn that Felix Marshal had seen. This was where the dog came out, turned over an empty box, and then waved a wand in her mouth to make Lafayette appear from the box. The box was carefully placed before the curtain went up. When Beauty turned it over by putting her paws on the edge, the box fell with the open bottom directly over a trap door in the stage. Then Lafayette magically appeared by coming up through the hole. The sides of the box kept the audience from seeing what was happening.

"The opening is good," Levy replied, pausing to light a fat cigar. After blowing a cloud of smoke, he added, "But that's not enough for a big-time show in New York. You've got to come up with something better."

Lafayette felt a cold chill. All he had wanted was to renew his vaudeville contract. Now Levy was talking about a big New York show. Although he had said that Lafayette's act was not good enough for this, the magician knew the talent scout had something in mind. Otherwise, he would not have mentioned New York.

"I am working on an idea to vanish Beauty out of a box," Lafayette said. "Also, Houdini told me about a trick a magician is doing in England. He sets up an easel on stage and draws a picture of a cocoon on it. The paper splits open, and a woman dressed like a moth comes out of the picture frame."

"I've heard of that," Levy said. "It is done by David Devant, a very fine magician."

"I can do the same idea, but change it to include Beauty," Lafayette went on. "I'll put up an easel, do a quick change to an artist character, and draw a doghouse on the paper. The paper splits, and Beauty jumps out of the frame. Where did she come from?"

Levy rolled the cigar in his mouth and said, "That'll be good. You should work those into your vaudeville act as soon as possible. But I'm thinking of something more grand.

"Adelaide Herrmann is carrying on the Alexander Herrmann show since her husband's death. Harry Kellar has got a really great magic show. Houdini's headed for the top with his wonderful escape tricks. And Burling Hull is doing well. There's a new man named Thurston who looks like a future star. Before you can hope to make the really big time, you have to come up with something *big.*"

Lafayette looked thoughtful. He rubbed Beauty's muzzle. Then he said slowly, "I was watching the Barnum & Bailey Circus a few weeks ago," he said. "I thought then that it might be possible to bring some of the color and spectacle of a circus onstage as background for a full evening's magic show."

Levy removed his cigar and smiled broadly. "Now you're talking!"

"It would cost a lot of money to stage," Lafayette replied.

"But it would make a lot of money if it were good."

"A vaudeville magician does not have a lot of money," Lafayette pointed out.

"If you can show the agency a really good plan for a magic spectacle, we can work out the money problem," Levy said. "The costumers will furnish costumes on credit if the agency will guarantee payment. You can get some spectacular sets the same way. You'll need a lot of support people. A really big magic show will probably need from fifteen to twenty people. The agency will pay them during the rehearsals. Then you can pay your troupe from the weekly theater returns."

"I'll do it!" Lafayette cried. "I cannot thank you en—"

"Wait!" Levy said, raising his hand. "I'm just thinking out loud. You first have to show that you can build such a show. Then we have to take the plan to theater owners to see if they will book another full evening's magic show. All this will take time.

"So you keep on with your vaudeville tour. Work out those new acts that bring the dog more into the show. That's a real audience grabber—the Magic Dog! Give her more to do. Make her a real magician and not just a prop for you. This is what makes your act so good now. The dog comes out and seems to make you appear herself. Do more of that."

He got up. "I got to run to catch my train. Keep improving the act. I'll keep an eye on you from time to time. This could be your big chance."

"We'll do it, Beauty and I, for we're partners!" Lafayette cried. "I can't thank you enough for giving us this chance."

Levy smiled. "Don't thank me. Thank the dog. She was the one who convinced me that the two of you could be real headliners."

6 * The Vanishing Dog

LAFAYETTE HAD BEEN a traveling performer for over ten years by this time. The talent scout had given him hope that he would at last move into big-time show business. However, he knew from sad experience that things did not always work out as planned. Luck would have as much to do with it as anything.

"Luck—and hard work," Lafayette told Beauty, talking to her as if she were human. "You've brought me luck. Now it's just plain hard work for both of us."

They continued with their regular show. After each performance, the man and dog would go to their hotel room. Here they would work for two hours before Lafayette went to bed. The secret of a good act is to rehearse until everything is perfect. No matter how hard it is to do, it must look smooth and easy to the audience.

One of the tricks they worked on was not for the stage. It was a "throwaway." They would do it in the streets to advertise their act.

Lafayette knew that many famous magicians had done this. Alexander Herrmann, who died in 1896, did this often. The talk it caused helped make him the most famous magician of his time. Harry Houdini was doing the same thing in a different way. He was visiting the local jail in each town where he played. He would challenge the police to lock him in a cell, from which he guaranteed to escape. A real showman, Houdini would insist on being put in the cell naked, so there would be no suspicion that he had a secret key or lock pick hidden on him. The magician always made good his boast to escape. This caused the tremendous publicity that would eventually make Houdini the most famous magician of all time.

Lafayette had seen Houdini do this once. Houdini never told how he managed to escape from the jail cell. However, Lafayette knew that the escape artist spent hours each day studying all kinds of locks. He knew exactly what to do to trip the latch on them all. Lafayette suspected, although he did not know for sure, that Houdini had a small steel lock pick stuck to the bottom of his bare foot when he was put naked into the cell.

Lafayette had a street trick of his own. It was one used by Herrmann the Great. Lafayette had gotten it from W. E. Robinson, who was an assistant to Alexander Herrmann for three years. The magician would take a small matchbox and seem to place two pennies in it. He would close the box and shake it so that the spectators could hear the coins clinking together inside. Then when he opened the box, the coins had vanished! The secret was simple. Lafayette never put the pennies in the box at all. While pretending to do so, he put the coins in his palm. He had another box with two coins in it fastened inside the cuff of his coat sleeve. When he raised his hand to shake the empty box, his audience heard the clink of the coins in the box in his sleeve and thought the sound came from the empty box the magician was showing them.

It was a good trick. Performed on a corner where a group might be waiting for a streetcar, it was excellent advertising for Lafayette's act. But now he wanted something in which Beauty could join him.

At the same time that he was trying to work out a street trick he could do with Beauty, Lafayette was also working with the dog on a stunt for the stage.

This was the Vanishing Dog turn that so mystified Felix Marshal when he saw the show in 1901. The trick itself was not a new one, but the dog made it seem different. It became the biggest hit in Lafayette's early shows with Beauty. At every show it drew more applause than the magical appearance of the bowl of water. The bowl imitation of Ching Ling Foo had been Lafayette's biggest crowd pleaser.

The Vanishing Dog trick was done with a special box. One side of the box was hinged. The magician could raise it to show the audience that the box was empty. Then the dog got in the box. The hinged side was closed. The magician turned the box around on its wheels to show there was no way the dog could slip out the back. The wheels raised it enough off the stage that the audience could see that the dog could not escape that way. Yet when the door was reopened seconds after it had been closed, the dog had vanished.

Worked with a human assistant, the trick was simple. The box had a double floor. The top of the floor was nailed to the back of the box to make an L shape. Although the back of the box appeared to be nailed to the top and sides, it was not. The L-shaped section that made up the false bottom and the back were attached by two steel pins. All the person inside had to do, once the door was closed so the audience could not see him, was to roll over and press his body against the backboard. His weight would cause it to move on the pins and fall back.

The false floor then became the back of the box. The back of the box became a ledge behind the box. The person to vanish would lie on this ledge. He would be out of the audience's sight while the magician opened the door again. He would appear to have vanished.

It was just as simple to reappear. The magician closed the box door. The vanished assistant then rolled over and put his weight on the false bottom. This caused the two sections to pivot again, returning to their original positions as floor and back of the box. When the magician opened the door, the assistant had mysteriously and magically reappeared.

The magician could then turn the box around to show there was nothing in the back. This trick can be done very rapidly. It only takes a split second for the assistant to roll over to appear or disappear.

The trick was easy with a human assistant, but it was much more difficult with a dog. Lafayette could not explain what he wanted to Beauty. He had to work out each part of the act, teaching the dog exactly what she was supposed to do.

He did this by guiding her through one portion at a time. Each time she was patted on the head, told how great she was, and given a bit of cookie—which she loved —when she did it right.

At the same time, he had to work out and teach Beauty her cues. These would silently tell her when to do what. It was slow work, but Beauty had above-average intelligence. She learned quickly. Even so it took Lafayette two months to work out the act. Part of the trouble was himself. He started out one way and then changed his ideas for the buildup. This confused Beauty for a while.

The actual disappearance part was not difficult. He began by teaching her to roll over when he snapped his fingers. Next she was taught to jump in the box on cue.

At this point he had trouble. Beauty was a freedom-loving dog. She did not like having the door closed when she was inside. Lafayette never got angry. He knew that animal training is mostly patience.

He gave up on closing the door for a time. He had her get in the box and gave the cue for her to roll over. Beauty, with the back of the box in her way, moved forward and rolled over as commanded. Patiently, Lafayette worked, petted, praised, and rewarded the dog until she understood. She was to jump in the box, stretch

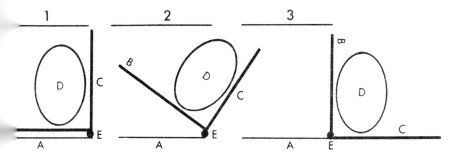

The Vanishing Box is a simple trick. In the above diagrams we are looking at the end of the box. A is the real floor of the box. B is a false floor that is attached to C, the back of the box. D is the object, person, or animal to be vanished. B and C pivot at point E. So when the front door is closed, Beauty or the person to be vanished leans heavily against the back C, and B and C swing over.

As shown in the third diagram, B becomes the new back of the box, and C, the old back, becomes a platform behind the box on which the vanished object lies, out of sight of the audience. By leaning back against B, the vanished animal or person can flip B and C back in their original positions and seem to reappear when the door is open.

An animal can be taught to roll over on cue and operate the box, but if the magician wishes to vanish an inanimate object, a spring catch can be built into the box so the magician can make the change without the audience's seeing him.

out against the backboard, and lean against the back as she rolled over. He showed her how several times by holding her in place and rolling her over against the pivoting back.

Once she understood, Beauty found it great fun to roll the back of the box over and put herself on the outside.

Lafayette next had to make the dog understand that she was to lie perfectly still once the swing of the backboard put her outside the box.

After this, Lafayette had to teach Beauty to let him close the door when she was inside. It was a full month before everything went exactly as Lafayette wanted it.

They were only half done then. He had to teach the dog to roll back inside when he gave her a cue. Next he had to work out the buildup to the act.

After a couple of false starts, he decided to let the audience think he was going to do a different trick. Then Beauty would take over and get in the box herself. He would order her to get out. She would shake her head and refuse.

It was all very carefully worked out and rehearsed many times in order for it to seem that Beauty was defying him. Actually, each move she made was in answer to a cue given her by Lafayette. Sometimes it was a snap of his fingers. Sometimes it was a certain word he emphasized in his patter. At other times it might be a certain way he waved his hand. Each of these cues told the dog to do a certain thing.

At least, this is the way it was in the beginning. Later, after they had worked the trick for a long time, Beauty knew her part so well that Lafayette no longer had to give her cues.

After two months, Lafayette thought the Vanishing Dog act was smooth enough to present to the public. Later, he could not remember the name of the city where the turn was introduced. He thought it might have been Richmond, Virginia.

Anyway, everything went perfectly smoothly for the first show. The applause was tremendous. Lafayette was so happy that he hugged Beauty until she yelped, after they got back to their dressing room.

However, all through Lafayette's life trouble immediately followed each success. The magician had worried about Beauty's ability to remember all her cues at the right time. He should have worried about himself instead of the dog. He was the one who messed things up.

The trouble came during the second performance of the Vanishing Dog trick. Lafayette had spotted the trick to close his portion of the show. By placing the best trick last, he could provide a steady buildup of wonders. He wanted people to leave the theater talking about The Great Lafayette and his wonderful dog. The best possible advertising for a show is a delighted person who tells others how great the show was.

The trick went along smoothly through the buildup. Then Lafayette, pretending to be angry at Beauty for not leaving the box, closed the door on her. He waved his wand and reopened the box to show that his magic had banished her.

At this point he was supposed to close the door and rap

on the box with his wand. This was Beauty's cue to roll back inside. Then he would turn the box around to show the audience that she had neither slipped out nor was hiding in the back.

He forgot to give the cue. He grabbed the box by its corner and spun it around. The surprised audience saw Beauty lying on the ledge. The spectators broke into loud laughter. Lafayette's face got red, but there was nothing he could do but laugh with the audience.

This was the only time they had trouble with the Vanishing Dog trick, although they had many difficulties with other tricks. This turn remained a favorite with Lafayette as long as he lived. Lafayette loved this trick above all others. He felt that it was the one that proved that he and Beauty could rise from vaudeville to a full evening's magic show.

Although they had bad luck with the Vanishing Dog trick in this city, it turned out to be a lucky stop for them. Lafayette happened to see a black man with small twin boys. He offered the man a job if he would bring the three-year-olds along with him.

This marked a great change for Lafayette. Earlier, he had had an assistant to help him make his quick clothing changes. But after the assistant stole some costumes from him, Lafayette refused to hire anyone else. He feared an assistant would steal his secrets and leave to start a competing show. But the possibilities of tricks using the twins were so great that the magician changed his mind.

The act that he worked up for the boys was one that

Alexander Herrmann had developed. After Herrmann's death, Adelaide Herrmann, his widow, presented it in her own show. In this act Beauty would take the place of the magician. He talked the idea over with Levy, the agent, who thought the combination of dog and children would be a winner.

Mrs. Herrmann's act was called The Flight of the Favorite. She had two cabinets raised on high legs. She stood between the cabinets and opened the door of the one on her right. It was empty. She closed the door and opened the one on the left. A small Japanese woman in a colorful kimono was in it. Mrs. Herrmann closed both doors. When she reopened them a second later, the Japanese woman had vanished from her cabinet and had mysteriously crossed the space to the other cabinet!

The two cabinets were five feet apart and five feet above the stage. It was impossible for the woman to have changed from one to the other. Except by magic, of course.

There are several ways this trick can be done. Adelaide Herrmann used "Black Art" (a clever technique invented by Max Ausinger, a German magician, in 1885). There was actually a girl in a Japanese costume in *both* cabinets *all the time.* The insides of the two boxes were painted a flat black. Each girl had a black velvet hood that could cover her entire body. Velvet does not cause reflections. So when the girl was entirely covered, the velvet hood blended with the black chamber. She could not be seen.

When Adelaide opened the doors to begin the trick,

one girl was covered with the velvet hood. The girl in the opposite chamber was uncovered. When the doors were closed for a second, the covered girl removed her hood. The girl in the opposite chamber put hers on.

It was as simple as that. But the trick was done so rapidly that the audience never had a chance to think about how it was done. The Queen of Magic, as she was called, had gone on to new wonders.

Lafayette had two small cabinets made for the twins. They were raised only a foot off the stage—just enough for the audience to see that the twins did not slip out through traps in the bottoms.

Lafayette merely introduced the trick and then left the stage. Thin wires ran from the door of each cabinet, so that Lafayette and the children's father could stand in the wings out of sight and pull the doors open. Springs caused them to close when the pull on the wires was relaxed. To the audience it seemed that the doors opened by magic.

Beauty acted as the magician in the act. She sat on her haunches between the cabinets. She barked. Both doors came open. The audience could see the child in one box. The other appeared empty. Beauty barked again. The doors magically closed. She barked and they reopened. The child had changed mysteriously to the other cabinet —or so it seemed.

Beauty caused the child to move from cabinet to cabinet several times. Then on the last opening of the door, the child vanished entirely.

For some reason, Lafayette used this trick only for one season. He never said why he dropped it. It was especially popular with children. In any event, it helped establish Beauty's reputation as a genuine dog magician.

7 ∗ On the Road

IT WAS A hard life traveling the vaudeville circuit in 1899. Often Lafayette and Beauty finished a show at midnight and rushed directly to the train station. They would sleep on the train. Arriving at dawn in a new town, they had to check in at a hotel and then hurry to the theater.

In the larger towns they might perform a full week. In the smaller towns their engagement might be for only one or two days. The one-night stand—as a single day's stop was called—was the worst. They spent almost all their time in the theater or on the train moving to the next engagement.

Life was a constant adventure. Once their train was derailed. Lafayette was frantic for fear they would miss their next performance. He was proud that he had never been late for a show. There was no chance to get the engine back on the tracks without several hours' delay.

Lafayette walked to a farm. He paid the farmer to drive them and their trunks of equipment into town. It was fifteen miles and slow going over a muddy road behind a team of tired mules. They arrived with only fifteen minutes to spare before their curtain call.

One time they did miss a scheduled performance. They were in the Midwest when a tornado swept in. Thunder and lightning split the sky. Torrential rain beat down on the speeding train. Lafayette was worrying about how they would get from the railroad station to their hotel without being drowned.

Then suddenly the train lurched as the engineer slammed on the air brakes. The screech of locked steel wheels against the rails was so loud that Lafayette heard it above the roar of the storm. The sudden stop threw him and Beauty off their seats. Lafayette hit his head against the side of the car. He got up shakily, more worried about Beauty than about himself.

After making sure that Beauty was unhurt, Lafayette went from his compartment to the coach. Passengers were picking themselves up from the aisles. Some were talking loudly; others were complaining even louder. Bundles from the overhead racks were scattered everywhere. A conductor came through the coaches, assuring everyone that there was no danger.

"The storm has washed out a bridge ahead of us," he said. "Fortunately, the engineer managed to stop in time."

"How long before we can go on?" someone asked.

"It will take quite a while to repair the trestle," the conductor said. "But another train will come from the junction to the other side of the break. As soon as the rain stops we'll cross the river on a barge, so everyone will not get soaked, and continue on the other train. It will probably take three hours or more."

Everyone sat back down and tried to make the best of the delay. Soon they began to get restless. Children were crying. Mothers were fretting. Men were complaining. Lafayette looked over the unhappy scene. Then he went back to his compartment.

"We were supposed to put on a show today," he told Beauty. "So we might as well do it, don't you think?"

He was pleased when Beauty barked. He honestly thought she understood every word he said.

"Of course," he went on, his voice sad, "we won't get paid for it, but if it helps people pass an uncomfortable time, maybe heaven will favor us."

Taking the dog in his arms, Lafayette walked down the aisle of the coach. He stopped and looked at a three-year-old boy who was crying loudly.

"If I give you a penny, will you stop crying?" Lafayette asked.

The boy, a little frightened by this strange man, cried louder.

"Oh!" Lafayette said. "You don't believe I have a penny. Well, I'll show you."

He put Beauty down on the seat beside the crying child.

"Look here," he said. "You'll see that I do have a penny. My friend, the Magic Dog, carries it for me."

He lifted up Beauty's floppy ear and seemed to take a penny from under it.

The little boy was so surprised he stopped crying in the middle of a "waaa"! He sat there with his mouth open, looking from the magician to the dog. People in the seats around them laughed. Others, farther back in the coach, stood up to see what all the merriment was about.

"Would you like to know how I did that?" Lafayette asked the boy. "Well, I will tell you. I am a magician! A real one, I'll have you know. And this"— Lafayette paused and bowed to Beauty, who bowed back—"this is my friend and my partner in magic. I am The Great Lafayette, and she is the Great Beauty."

Lafayette turned to face the rest of the coach. "You don't believe me! I can see it in your faces. Well, since we can't do anything except sit here and growl at each other, I'll take the time to prove to you that my friend and I are real magicians."

He walked to the front of the car. He noted happily that all the crying and complaining had stopped. Everyone in the coach was watching him.

He asked two men sitting in the front seat to move for a little while. Then he took some suitcases from the overhead rack and piled them beside the seat so that the valises and the back of the seat made a screen behind which he could duck.

Next he borrowed a derby hat from a man. He asked

a woman to lend him her shawl and hat. He took them and disappeared behind the screen he had made. In his pockets were many small things he had put there before leaving his compartment.

In the second or two he was out of sight, Lafayette put on the derby and stuck a fake mustache, taken from his loaded pocket, under his nose. When he rose up so the audience could see him, he was no longer Lafayette. He was a tough Irish politician.

He ducked back out of sight. When he reappeared almost instantly, a different mustache and a different angle of his hat turned him into a pawnbroker.

But the next quick change was what made the entire coachful break into uproarious laughter. This time he only raised his head and shoulders above the back of the seat. His body was hidden. Lafayette had put on the woman's hat. He had drawn the shawl up around his neck, hunched his shoulders, and pursed his lips. He looked for all the world like a little old grandmother.

The passengers broke into loud applause. Lafayette claimed to dislike people, but he loved attention. Applause made him work harder than ever to please his audience. Beauty also loved applause. She barked happily. Years later a writer said that the dog was such a ham that all one had to do was clap one's hands and Beauty would take a bow!

Lafayette returned the borrowed hats and shawl. After handing the hat back to the woman, he stopped and looked uneasy.

"Excuse me, madame," he said. "I think there's something—"

He took the hat and appeared to pull from it a little mouse, which he held up by the tail. It was made of rubber, but a slight jerk on the rubber tail as he held it up made the toy seem real.

He returned the hat with his left hand and kept dangling the rubber mouse by the tail with the other.

"Now what in the world will I do with *you*?" he asked the mouse. Then his face brightened. "After all, I *am* a magician. Why don't I just make you—"

At this point he flipped his hand. "Vanish!" he cried. The mouse disappeared.

Then quickly, one after another, he brought a coin seemingly out of the air and then made it vanish again. He pulled a cigar out of the air and presented it to a man nearby. Then he showed his empty hands, put his palms together, and rubbed briskly. When he opened his hand, he held a small red rubber ball.

He made it disappear and then reappear. Then he held it up for all to see.

"You know," he said. "I can make just about anything vanish. Coins, cigars, dogs, chairs, houses, and even—"

He paused and looked hard at a small boy sitting beside his mother on a seat halfway down the coach. "And even naughty boys!"

The passengers laughed, but the boy slipped down in his seat and moved closer to his mother.

Lafayette enclosed the red ball in his hands, hiding it

from his audience. When he opened his hands, the ball had changed colors. It was then a yellow ball. He held it up for all to see.

"Although I can vanish just about everything else, I cannot, for the life of me, make a yellow ball vanish. Strange, isn't it! Also, it is very sad. It is impossible to have a real magic show and not make a *yellow* ball disappear. Fortunately, I am saved, because although I cannot make a yellow ball vanish, my friend and my partner, the Great Beauty, can do it for me!"

He turned and bowed to the dog. She barked back at him. She was standing on her hind legs on the coach seat. Her paws were on the back of the seat.

"Are you ready, Beauty? Very well, I shall throw the ball into the air. You order it to vanish when you wish."

Lafayette threw the ball into the air. "There it goes!" he cried as the ball left his hand. It went up almost to the ceiling of the coach and fell back into his outstretched hand.

He repeated this seven times, crying, "There it goes!" each time he tossed the ball into the air. The eighth time he brought his hand up and cried, "There it goes!" Beauty barked.

"It's gone!" Lafayette cried.

It appeared to the audience that the ball had vanished in midair!

There were cries of astonishment from the audience. Lafayette smiled. He quickly went into another trick before the spectators could realize that they had been *re-*

ally tricked. On the final toss of his hand, when the ball was made to disappear, it never left his hand. He threw his hand up as if to toss the ball and cried, "There it goes!" The spectators, having seen the ball go up before at the same cry, thought they saw it again. Then when the magician cried, "It's gone!" they believed that too.

This is a very old trick, practiced by most of the great magicians at one time or another. It rarely fails to work. In this case, the illusion that Beauty made the ball disappear with her bark was very skillfully done.

When the storm stopped and they finally were able to go on to their destination, the passengers spread the word about the show Lafayette and Beauty had put on for them. This was splendid advertising that helped pack the theater when they finally appeared.

Their adventures continued. In one town the hotel where they were staying caught on fire. Beauty's barking awoke Lafayette. The two fled from the burning building.

There is no doubt that Beauty saved Lafayette's life in this case. Fire spreads quickly through the dry wood of old hotels. Beauty's alarm enabled Lafayette to get out early. However, in later years Lafayette liked to embellish the stories he told.

According to him, Beauty raced down the hall, barking a warning at every door. He credited her with saving every person on the floor. Still later, he claimed that a baby had been left in a room. Beauty rushed in and grabbed the child's nightdress in her teeth. She pulled the baby down the hall to safety.

Magicians' stories, like their tricks, are often bigger—much bigger—than life!

The Great Lafayette and Beauty were becoming more popular the longer they performed. Levy, the talent scout for the Keith circuit, looked in on the show again later in the season. He did not let Lafayette know that he was in the audience. He just watched the act and the people in the theater. Then he left quietly to make his report back in New York.

One of the things that impressed him was how skillfully Lafayette and Beauty handled angry people in the audience. It was part of Lafayette's act at this time to step down into the audience and seem to pull an odd article from the clothing or person of some man or woman. This was very popular, for often the person was someone many of the audience knew.

Lafayette tried to size up the persons he picked. He wanted those who would laugh at the joke. However, he sometimes made a mistake. The night Levy was in the audience Lafayette noticed a gray-haired woman sitting on an aisle seat. She had a large handbag in her lap. It was partially open, for she had a cold and kept taking a handkerchief from it to wipe her nose.

This was ideal for Lafayette. She was on the aisle where she could be easily seen, and the partially opened bag provided a good prop for what he wanted to do.

He went over to a man sitting on the opposite side of

the aisle. He did his old trick of seeming to pull a cigar from under the man's beard. This he presented to the man, who laughed as loudly as the rest of the audience.

Then Lafayette crossed the aisle to the woman. He smiled at her and reached down to her bag. He appeared to take a large bone from the bag.

"Is this a present you have brought for my partner Beauty?" he asked.

The audience laughed, but the woman turned red with anger. She stood up and shook her finger in Lafayette's face. In a loud voice she denounced him for making a woman old enough to be his mother look ridiculous.

Lafayette tried to apologize. She would not listen. She kept on lecturing him on his bad manners. The audience was enjoying it hugely, but Lafayette was not. His face was red with embarrassment and anger. The audience was laughing *at* him, and he hated it. Also, he knew that the theater manager would be angry. Managers disliked performers who angered patrons. After all, the performer would move on after the engagement ended, but the patron remained in the town. She might never come back to the theater again.

"I've got to do something to get her in a good humor again," Lafayette thought as he went back to the stage.

By the time he got to the stage, an idea had occurred to him. It was triggered by a young woman standing in the wings. She was a member of a dancing team that would follow Lafayette and Beauty on the show bill.

Asking the audience to excuse him for one moment,

Lafayette stepped quickly into the wings. The woman was holding a bouquet of roses that figured in her dance.

"Please," Lafayette said to her, "let me have just one rose, and I'll be your admirer for life!"

As a trouper herself, she understood that Lafayette was trying to do something to cover up his mistake. She let him take a rose from the bouquet. He took it back on stage and cued Beauty to sit up. He handed her the rose. She took the stem in her mouth. He cued her to follow him. Together they went back down in the audience. All Beauty's actions were done in answer to cues that were contained in movements of Lafayette's hands—movements that seemed quite ordinary to the audience.

They went up to the angry woman. Beauty sat up on her hind legs and raised her head to present the rose to the woman. The audience broke into very loud applause. The woman looked astonished. Then she smiled and took the rose the dog was offering her.

The applause grew louder. Lafayette and Beauty both bowed to the lady. Then they returned to the stage. There Lafayette's eyes sought out the woman. She was still smiling and holding the rose.

Over a year later, when he was in New York, Lafayette received a small package from this woman. It was a small sweater she had knitted for Beauty. She wrote a short note thanking the dog for the rose. Then she added to Lafayette, "But I still think that *you* are a very impertinent young man!"

8 * The Lion's Bride

THE YEAR 1900 opened with a bang. It was the start of a new century. The United States was on the march. Business was booming, and the country looked forward to great prosperity. The happy people packed the theaters, and Lafayette was one of those who profited.

The success he achieved on the Keith vaudeville circuit with Beauty in 1899 helped him get his own full evening magic show. He remembered what Levy, the talent scout, had told him. From the first he made his show bigger and more spectacular than the shows of the other magicians.

One writer said that Lafayette's big show was more circus than a stage show. In this he was right, for it was a circus that gave Lafayette the idea for the hair-raising stunt that made his show the talk of the town. It was an act that twice almost got him and Beauty killed and that did lead to Lafayette's death eleven years later.

In 1899—the year before—Lafayette had gone to a performance of the Barnum & Bailey Circus. He was thinking about adding the character of clown to the quick-change part of his vaudeville act. However, once inside the circus tent, Lafayette was more interested in the lion tamer than in the clowns. He was fascinated at the way the daring man, armed with only a whip and a kitchen chair, went into the cage with the wild beasts.

After the show, Lafayette went back to talk to the performer. He introduced himself as a magician who was thinking of adding a lion-vanishing act to his show.

The circus man was willing to talk. "I know," he told Lafayette, "that the banners out front call me a lion *tamer,* but there is no such thing. These big cats are never 'tamed.' They are wild and remain wild. I am a lion *trainer."*

"Then they are always dangerous?" Lafayette asked.

"Yes," the circus man replied. "If you try to work with a lion in your act, you are asking for trouble."

He unfastened the gold buttons of the scarlet jacket he wore in his act. Then he stripped off his undershirt. Lafayette saw that the upper part of the man's body was a mass of scars.

"I have worked the big cats all my life," the lion trainer said. "I understand them. I am wary of them. I am careful when I'm in their cages. But they still were able to do this to me. No matter how careful you are, you'll make a mistake sooner or later. When you do—the lion is going to be on you with fangs and claws."

"I want to do it anyway," Lafayette said slowly.

The mass of scars on the animal trainer's body gave him a sick feeling. At the same time they increased his determination. That night he sat up late in his hotel room and worked out the details of the lion act he hoped to feature in his full evening show—if he ever got one.

The trick proved more difficult that he first imagined. He could not get it ready for the shows he put on in 1900. The New York theaters closed down in midsummer because of the heat. This was before air conditioning. Lafayette spent this time working on problems in the act that he had already named the Lion's Bride.

He rented a lion from a dealer who supplied wild animals to circuses. The lion was old and sleepy. He would not stand up and roar as Lafayette wanted him to do. The magician complained to the dealer who had rented him the beast.

"I'll fix that," the man said.

He rigged up a metal plate in the bottom of the lion's cage. Then an electric cord was attached to the plate and connected to an electrical socket. A rheostat was placed in the line to reduce the amperage. When the switch was thrown, the lion received a mild shock that caused him to roar angrily.

Lafayette was delighted, but doubtful. "Does it hurt the lion?"

The dealer assured him that the shock was too mild to injure the animal. "If it hurt the beast," he said, "I would not do it, because my animals are valuable. I lose money if I injure one."

With this assurance, Lafayette used the electrical shock to make the tired old beast seem ferocious.

It wasn't long after this that the magician learned the lion trainer had been right when he warned Lafayette that lions never become tame. The lion was asleep, resting his head against the bars of the cage. Lafayette walked by. He carelessly came too close to the cage. The big cat sensed his nearness. Moving with a cat's lightning speed, the lion jabbed a paw through the bars.

Lafayette was just a fraction of an inch too far away, and the wild beast's claw only caught the shoulder of his coat. Even so, the jerk of the claws in the cloth pulled the magician around. He lost his balance and fell. His head hit the stage. He was momentarily stunned and within reach of the lion's claws.

But in the split second when the lion's paw first caught the magician's coat, Beauty leaped forward, barking and snarling. The lion, distracted by the unexpected noise, turned to see what new threat faced him. He lunged against the bars, but Beauty sprang back, still barking wildly.

This gave two frightened stagehands time to run forward and drag Lafayette to safety.

While the magician was always ready to build up Beauty's part and give the dog more credit than she deserved, this is one time when all credit was due her. She showed bravery, intelligence, and loyalty of a high degree. She certainly saved Lafayette's life in this instance.

The theater manager advised the magician to drop the lion act. But Lafayette was stubborn. Also, he knew that it would give him a fantastic attraction. It would be more breathtaking than anything that Leon Herrmann (Alexander's nephew), Adelaide Herrmann, or Harry Kellar —another famous magician—had in their magic acts.

So he continued to work on the problems through the rest of 1900 and 1901. He finally introduced the act in New York in 1902. It was the sensation he had expected it to be.

As the act was worked out, the lion was in a long cage. A separate set of bars, which could be raised, separated the large cage into two small cages. The lion was in the back cage.

The stage was decorated like a circus tent. All kinds of entertainers, jugglers, acrobats, and clowns passed in front of the lion's cage.

Then as the colorful parade of people moved away, Lafayette came out dressed as an Oriental monarch. He was dragging a frightened girl. He loudly cried that if she would not marry him, he would make her the bride of the lion. She refused, of course. Otherwise there would have been no show.

Lafayette handed the girl to two assistants who were dressed as Oriental slaves. They opened the door of the cage. The girl, who wore a wedding dress, was shoved into the front cage. Only the partition of bars separated her from the lion.

As soon as the "slaves" locked her inside, they grasped

ropes attached to overhead pulleys so they could raise the bars separating her and the lion.

Lafayette, standing with his back to the audience, gave the signal. The stage assistants strained at their ropes. The bars lifted. The girl screamed wildly, her voice echoing through the hushed theater.

At that moment the lion roared on cue—stimulated by a charge of electricity from the plate in the floor of its small cage.

The lion reared up on its hind legs, springing at the defenseless girl. Then in midspring the lion stopped. Its paws lifted off its head!

And there was The Great Lafayette, in his most startling quick-change act, inside a lion's suit!

The act was a sensation. To the audience, it seemed impossible. There was absolutely no question about its being a real lion in that cage. They had seen it move and roar. No one, regardless of how clever, could put on a lion's skin and move like that.

Also, Lafayette had been *outside* the cage with the girl. He had delivered the girl to the slaves to be put in the cage, but he had remained there in full view of the audience while the girl was forced inside the bars.

Lafayette was standing outside the cage, dressed as the Pasha, when he gave the signal to raise the bars and let the lion into the section occupied by the terrified princess. But in the instant that the lion sprang, Lafayette had somehow managed miraculously to move from the Pasha's costume to the real lion's cage. There he had to remove the real lion, and then crouch down with a fake head and skin to take the lion's place.

It was *impossible* to do in the short time allowed for this part of the act. Everyone agreed that this was true. Yet it had been done! How? By magic, of course, but it was old magic. There was not one single action in this amazing act that was new. Everything in it was standard conjuring. All Lafayette did was to put tricks employed by almost every magician together in a brilliant display of showmanship that bewildered and delighted his audiences.

Because of the way he put the act together, Lafayette not only fooled his audience but many of his fellow magicians as well. The secret was rooted in his extraordinary quick-change ability, but the real secret would not be revealed until after Lafayette's death in a theater fire in Edinburgh, Scotland.

His death created another mystery that had people shaking their heads as they had over his amazing acts. But all this was still nine years in the future when The Great Lafayette bewildered the people of New York with his brilliant Lion's Bride act.

The Lion's Bride was so popular that Lafayette kept improving the act. He got rid of the circus tent he'd used earlier. Instead, he turned the act into a short play set in a Turkish palace. The girl became a Christian princess. In its final form, the Lion's Bride was very involved and much more bewildering.

The princess is captured by the evil Pasha, who threatens to throw her in the lion's cage if she does not marry him. Lafayette plays the role of the Pasha.

The captive has a dog (Beauty, of course) which had been given to her by her sweetheart, a brave Persian officer. The girl sends the dog to take a message to the Persian. Beauty eludes the guards who try to kill her and finds the Persian (also played by Lafayette).

The hero comes to rescue the girl, but the Pasha traps him and the princess in a room in the castle. In desperation to save his sweetheart, Lafayette (as the Persian) puts on her wedding gown and heavy veil. Acting on the Pasha's orders, the guards seize him, thinking he is the princess.

At this point the audience is really bewildered. They know that Lafayette is the Pasha, but he is also hidden in the bride's clothing. How could he be in two places at once? Lafayette does not give them time to puzzle much about it. The show continues.

The Pasha orders the Bride to be thrown to the lion. The victim is put in the cage, separated from the lion by the partition of bars. The lion, goaded by the electrical shock, roars on cue. The Pasha laughs evilly. He signals for the slaves to raise the bars separating the ferocious beast from its cringing victim.

The lion rears up to attack the bride. Beauty rushes forward, barking as she bravely tries to help. Then the "lion" jerks off its head and—as in the original act—is revealed as The Great Lafayette in an animal suit.

"*Three* Lafayettes on the stage at *one* time? Well, it

looked that way!" wrote one critic. "And that is the heart of stage magic: to make something look like what it is not!"

The Lion's Bride was very popular, but it caused Lafayette trouble to the day of his death. In 1902, during a show in Brooklyn, New York, Lafayette was injured during the act.

The cage was like those used by lion tamers in circuses. The real lion's section was a permanent cage. The cage for the bride was made of sections of steel bars that could be dismantled for ease in shipping from one town to another. During the Brooklyn show, the front section with the door came loose. Lafayette was hit on the head and knocked unconscious. The show had to be canceled and the audience's money refunded.

Then a year later, Lafayette was almost killed in Indianapolis, Indiana. By this time he had bought another dog to be a companion for Beauty. This dog lacked Beauty's intelligence. Just before the show, as the lion's cage was rolled into position behind the backdrop, the dog slipped through the bars into the drowsy lion's cage.

The lion suddenly came to life. It sprang, catching the yelping dog in its teeth. Lafayette grabbed up a whip and a chair—the standard lion trainer's equipment—and went into the cage.

Lafayette was as brave as a trainer, but he lacked the skill.

The lion released the dog and sprang at the man. Lafayette held the chair in front of him and snapped the whip. The lion caught the chair with a slash of his paw. He leaped upon the magician before Lafayette could run. Lafayette hit the floor. He was unconscious. The lion crouched over him. The man's chest was bleeding where the animal's claws had ripped through his clothing.

Beauty once again came to her partner's rescue. She darted into the cage, yelping wildly. As far as size was concerned, this was like a child attacking a grown man.

Even so, it worked. The lion, its fangs bared to sink into the unconscious man, hesitated and turned its head to snarl at the barking dog.

Slight as the time was, this gave the stagehands a chance to grab poles. They stuck these through the bars, jabbing the infuriated lion and driving him back from the still body of the magician. Then they quickly pulled him out.

A doctor was hastily summoned. Lafayette's chest had been raked by the lion's claws, and he had been bitten on the shoulder. The wounds were painful, and he had lost some blood. There was also a bad bruise on his head where he was knocked unconscious when he struck the floor of the cage.

Lafayette held Beauty in his arms while he was being bandaged. The dog seemed to feel her partner's pain, for she whimpered as the doctor wound bandages about the magician's body. Lafayette stroked her head.

"My friend! My friend!" he said in a choked voice.

Then to the doctor he said, "She is the guardian of my life! If I lost her, I would not live a week!"

Lafayette was a true prophet when he said this, although his time was wrong. Actually, the magician only lived five days longer than Beauty.

The doctor tried to get Lafayette to go to the hospital. The magician, although weak and shaky, insisted on going on with the show.

As it was, the show was delayed forty-five minutes. The audience was told what had happened. They had their choice of waiting until Lafayette could be bandaged and start the show or receiving their money back. Not a single person asked for the refund. They all stayed.

Lafayette came onstage, walking unsteadily. He carried Beauty in his arms. He received thunderous applause. To increase the drama of the moment, the curtain forming the backdrop was drawn. This was to permit the audience to see the caged lion that had almost killed the magician.

Still holding Beauty in his arms, Lafayette told the audience the story of what had happened. Of course, being a magician and a stage performer, he enlarged on the truth. Instead of just barking as she actually did, in Lafayette's story the courageous dog attacked the ferocious lion to save her fellow magician's life.

9 *The Dog Star

LAFAYETTE AND BEAUTY were now on the road to fame and fortune. Lafayette kept increasing the size of his show. He had forty people working for him. It took three railroad cars to carry the cast and props when he toured the country. He and Beauty were stars now, and they acted like stars.

Beauty had her own room set apart on Lafayette's private railroad car. The advance agent for the show traveled several days ahead of the rest to make all arrangements. His orders were to see that the hotels where they were booked would accept Beauty. The dog was now so well known that the request was never refused.

Lafayette remembered bitterly the early days when he could not get Beauty into his hotel rooms. He bragged now about the high-class hotels that accepted her. He even had a leather collar made for the dog. It was studded with silver tags on which Lafayette had engraved the names of the famous hotels where she stayed.

After his enormous success in the United States, Lafayette took his show to London. He rented a house in London. He had a sign placed over the front door where all passersby could read it: "THE MORE I SEE OF PEOPLE, THE MORE I LOVE MY DOG."

Any of the forty people he hired was immediately fired if Beauty took a dislike to him or her. He had two servants who followed behind him when he walked the streets. They were required to salute both their master and Beauty when they reported for work.

Lafayette bought an expensive car. He had the hood ornament removed and replaced with a small silver image of Beauty. She had an American flag in her mouth.

This led one writer to say, "All magicians are odd, but The Great Lafayette is the oddest of them all!"

Lafayette opened his show in England as soon as he had it running smoothly. It took courage for him to do this. The greatest magicians of the time performed or had performed recently in London. Lafayette's show would be judged in competition with the best. Maskelyne and Devant, two of the great conjurers of all time, had a permanent magic show at London's Egyptian Hall. Londoners still remembered the great shows of Alexander and Adelaide Herrmann, and Alexander's famous brother, Compars (Carl) Herrmann. Buatier de Kolta, one of the great inventors of magic tricks, surprised everyone with his Vanishing Bird Cage trick and his new way of making a woman vanish.

Also, many Londoners still recalled the great magicians of the past. They had seen Jean Robert-Houdin of

France; Anderson, the Great Wizard of the North; the fabulous Signor Blitz, the Laughing Magician; and other famous men from the history of magic.

Yet, this man, who only three years before had been a second-rate vaudeville artist, opened with a show that had all London cheering.

The memory of this show was still fresh in the mind of Sidney W. Clark, a well-known British writer, when he noted seventeen years after Lafayette's death:

> Lafayette took his audiences from surprise to surprise so rapidly that they had no time to think whether what they saw was legerdemain or mere bluff. A crowded stage, many assistants, and magnificent setting and dress, all impressed the eye, and concealed the fact that as a conjurer Lafayette was by no means in the front rank.
>
> As a showman, he was easily first. He was blessed with a personality, a love of color and a sense of mystery, that put him far ahead, as an entertainer, of other more capable conjurers. . . .

Lafayette opened in London's Hippodrome, a new showplace built to house circuses and very large entertainments. An ordinary magic show would have been lost in the huge place. Lafayette filled it with motion and spectacle.

Beauty had her part to play in the grand show. But she was so small that she was lost in the fast action. Lafayette called the show "The Carnival of Magic." It was a carnival. In fact, it was practically a circus.

There was nothing really new in the show. Lafayette just presented variations of old acts on a larger, grander, and more spectacular scale.

Before he had been content to produce a bowl of water from under his cape or to make Beauty materialize from a sheet of paper drawn in the shape of a doghouse. Now he followed wonder with more wonders.

Coming out as Ching Ling Foo, he waved his scarf over a low table. There was the familiar bowl of water. He waved the cloth again. The water had disappeared from the bowl. He waved again and a chicken jumped out of the bowl and ran squawking across the stage. Next he again hid the bowl with a wave of his cloth. The bowl disappeared. In its place was Beauty with a wand in her mouth. She moved to the other end of the table, sat up on her haunches and moved her head to wave the wand.

As Beauty waved the magic wand, Lafayette flipped his scarlet cloth. When it dropped, a five-year-old child stood on the table.

After the applause stopped, Beauty dropped the wand from her mouth and barked at Lafayette. He looked at her in surprise and then glanced in a shamefaced manner at the audience.

"I'm so sorry!" he said.

Beauty picked up the wand again. She waved it. Lafayette flipped the cloth in front of the child. The audience expected the boy to disappear. Instead, when the scarlet cloth dropped, the boy had doubled! There were now *two* of him!

These were, of course, the twins who had joined the show when Lafayette hired their father back in his vaudeville days. The audience did not know this, and Lafayette did not give them time to think about it. The wave of

Beauty's wand had cloned the child long before the word "clone" was invented. The show then moved immediately into a new wonder, leaving the audience no time to puzzle out the rather obvious secrets of the last marvel they had seen.

A special feature that set Lafayette's Carnival of Magic off from other conjuring shows was the magician's truly outstanding ability to change costumes and character in a split second. All through the Hippodrome show he kept changing from one character to another. In one act he was the Chinese Ching Ling Foo. Next he was an artist, wearing a beret and a flowing tie. He splashed paint on some boards, using a very large brush. It was nothing but a group of colored spots. Then these boards were placed on an upright turntable and spun rapidly. The spots blended together to produce a landscape painting of a mountain and lake.

The Bride of the Lion, of course, still remained the most popular of the many acts that Lafayette presented. No one could puzzle out the secret of how the magician could be three different people at the same time.

However, after coming to England, Lafayette built another act that was almost as popular as the lion switch. This was "Doctor Kremser." The magician got the idea from a popular play by George du Maurier called *Trilby.* The play was about an evil hypnotist who turned a beautiful girl into a great singer.

Lafayette used only the hypnotist, calling him Dr. Kremser. For the first time, the magician wove a message into one of his acts. At that time medical people were using dogs to experiment in different types of operations. These vivisectionists—as they were called—enraged Lafayette. Because of his great love for Beauty, the thought of anyone operating on a dog as an experiment filled him with loathing and horror.

The program for Lafayette's show gives the outline of the one-act play:

Dr. Kremser, the great hypnotic surgeon and vivisectionist, is faced with a terrible problem.

His only daughter is on the point of death. She suffers from a mysterious disease, for which there is no known treatment. There is a new operation that might help her, but it has never been tried. He realizes that the only way to find out if the operation works is to try it out on his faithful dog.

It is night when he comes to this decision. There is no way he can find another animal. He shudders at the thought of practicing on his own dear canine companion. But it is a question between his own flesh and blood and that of a dog. He decides against the dog.

He orders a servant to prepare the dog for the operation. The servant pleads for the life of the dog. The doctor hypnotizes the servant, who then arranges the vivisection table for the operation.

The doctor is preparing the anaesthetic to keep the animal quiet during the operation. Suddenly the chemicals overpower him. Dr. Kremser falls to the ground. Then does he pass through a series of strange tortures. . . .

The doctor's tortures are shown to the audience in a series of magical appearances and disappearances. A human figure with a dog's head appears out of a flash of smoke. Dr. Kremser rises from the floor and screams as the dog-headed human threatens him with the same knife he intended to use on the dog.

As he screams, the monster disappears in a burst of smoke. The doctor turns slowly, looking at the empty vivisection table. The dog—which is Beauty, of course—appears on the table. As Dr. Kremser shakily picks up the knife dropped by the dog-headed man, he turns toward the dog, but there is a flash of light and his daughter—wearing the nightdress from her sickbed—appears mysteriously. She pleads for the dog's life.

Kremser drops the knife and rushes to clasp the girl in his arms. She vanishes. In her place, the dog-headed person reappears.

The monster grabs up the vivisection knife and cuts off Dr. Kremser's head! The monster turns, holding the doctor's head by its hair. A blazing furnace suddenly appears in the back of the room. The doctor's head is hurled into it. His headless body lies on the floor for the horrified audience to see.

At this terrible moment, a door opens at stage right. The daughter walks in. She is real this time. The fever has broken. Having heard the doctor's scream as he was being beheaded, she has rushed to the laboratory. She kneels beside her stricken father.

Dr. Kremser then gets up. His head has been miraculously restored—to the audience's surprise. Now the audience learns that the foregoing had all been a nightmare suffered by the doctor after he was put to sleep by the anesthetic accident.

Beauty comes in, sitting up to lick his hand. The doctor picks up the vivisection knife and hurls it through the window. He then enfolds both his daughter and Beauty in his arms as the curtain falls to close the act.

The act was bloodthirsty and horrifying, but the audiences loved it. Cutting off the head of a person, animal, or bird is a very old trick. The first mention of it is in an Egyptian papyrus more than three thousand years old. There are several ways of doing the trick. They all use a lifelike dummy head of the person whose head is cut off. Lafayette used Black Art in making the people appear and disappear.

Although Dr. Kremser thrilled the audiences, Lafayette's decapitation was not nearly as clever as the one performed by Maskelyne and Cooke in London's Egyptian Hall before Cooke's retirement.

The two magicians got into a violent argument. Maskelyne grabbed a knife and sliced at Cooke's neck. In doing so, he momentarily blocked the audience's view of Cooke, who was seated in a chair. In this brief second, Maskelyne dropped a black velvet hood over his partner's head. At the same time he grabbed by the hair a wax image of Cooke's head, which was hidden behind Cooke's body. Then Maskelyne stepped back, holding the fake head by its hair. The black hood over the other magician's head blended with the black velvet backdrop. It appeared to the audience that the head was missing.

All such acts, performed through the centuries, had been gruesome. However, Maskelyne and Cooke added a touch of comedy that changed their version from a horror show to a comedy.

Maskelyne put the fake head down on a table. Cooke's headless body got out of its chair, picked up the head and tucked it under his arm, and stalked off the stage. The black velvet background was arranged so that the hood over his real head blended with the backdrop as he walked from the stage. It looked as if the headless body were carrying its own head away.

Then just before he exited from the stage, Cook would pause. The head under his arm looked straight at the audience with supposedly lifeless eyes. Then one eye (operated by a secret spring pushed by Cooke's hand) closed in a wink at the audience!

Following his highly successful Hippodrome show, Lafayette and Beauty took the Carnival of Conjuring on a tour of the English provinces. The show was very successful, but not as spectacular as the London show had been. This was because the theater stages were not as large.

In the Hippodrome show, Lafayette changed his drum major impersonation to an imitation of John Philip Sousa, the famous March King and author of "The Stars and Stripes Forever." In the costume of Sousa, Lafayette led the entire seventy-five piece Hippodrome orchestra in a rousing march around the huge stage.

However, the smaller theaters were a better showcase for the acts in which Beauty was involved. The audiences loved the Magic Dog. Lafayette glowed with pride at her success. He never tired of telling all who would listen about the times she had saved his life.

Naturally those who listened to Lafayette's tales believed that they were as much illusion as his acts on stage. Then in Turnly, England, during one of his tours, the lion got loose during a performance of the Lion's Bride. What happened next did not prove that Lafayette's other stories were true, but it did prove that they could have been.

The lion broke some bars loose in his cage. He leaped out. Lafayette's assistants fled. By that time, Lafayette had learned a lot about handling wild animals. He grabbed a chair in one hand and a whip in the other. He put himself between the lion and the audience as professionally as any real lion trainer.

The audience, used to excitement on Lafayette's stage, thought all this was part of the show. No one got up and ran. This was fortunate, for a panic would have caused many to be trampled in the crush.

With Beauty barking wildly to draw the lion's attention from Lafayette, the magician advanced upon the lion. He held the chair by its back, with the legs pointed toward the beast, in the manner of trainers.

The lion roared and slapped at the chair. Lafayette shouted and hit him across the nose with the whip. The lion roared again, turning his head uncertainly from Lafayette to the barking dog.

Then slowly he began backing up. Lafayette came in closer. The lion, still faced with the whip and chair, backed into the cage. Lafayette upturned a table on the set and pushed it against the break in the bars.

Then he went on with the regular show. The audience applauded loudly, not knowing that this was not part of the act until they read about it in their newspapers the next day.

10 * Fame and Fortune

AT THIS TIME London more than any other city in the world was the heart of the theatrical world. There was more glory in a successful London run than there would have been in New York, Paris, or any of the other famous cities of the world.

In spite of the number of magicians who performed there, London took Lafayette and Beauty to its heart. Between 1901 and 1903, Lafayette and his canine partner traveled between America and England. Then, in 1903, he bought a fine house in Tavistock Square and made London his permanent home.

Here, Beauty had her own room, complete with bath. She was truly the mistress of the house. If she showed dislike of any servant, that person was fired.

Although he claimed to hate people and to be without a friend in the world except for Beauty, Lafayette entertained often in his home. His parties were always well attended by the famous as well as by the unknown. However, if Beauty acted as if she did not like someone, that person was asked to leave.

Lafayette made his position clear in a sign he had put up in his drawing room: "YOU MAY EAT MY FOOD, YOU MAY COMMAND MY SERVANTS, BUT YOU *MUST* RESPECT MY DOG!"

As a result, they said of him in England as they had spoken of him in America: "The Great Lafayette is a little *odd*!" This oddness did not prevent crowds from flocking to his show. Perhaps it even helped attendance. By 1910 Lafayette was the highest-paid magician in England. He, however, denied this. He claimed his annual income was only half of what was reported. "The other half," he would say, "belongs to my partner, Beauty."

The magician had acquired other dogs, among them a Dalmatian he called Mabel. But none was loved as he loved Beauty.

Beauty was growing old as The Great Lafayette's fame increased. She no longer had the pep of former years and liked to lie in a warm place and sleep more. As a result, she did not play as large a part in the show as she once had. However, she was onstage every performance in one act or another. She always took the final bow with Lafayette at the conclusion of the show.

For a while Beauty was part of the famous "Teddy Bear" act. In 1903, former United States President Theodore Roosevelt was on a hunting trip. He and members of his party surprised a bear. They raised their guns to shoot when a tiny cub ran out to join its mother. Roosevelt put down his gun and shouted for the others not to shoot the mother bear. A United States newspaper carried a large cartoon showing "Teddy" stopping a hunter from shooting the mother and her cub.

A toy company immediately came out with a cute stuffed bear, which it named the "Teddy bear" in honor of "Teddy" Roosevelt. The teddy bear is still with us today, although many have forgotten how the little bear got its name.

As a result of the publicity, Lafayette introduced a teddy bear in his show. At the beginning of the skit, Lafayette took the bear from its box. A large metal key was used to wind it up and the bear made several jerky, mechanical somersaults across the stage. Then the comedy started.

Lafayette wanted to put the bear back in its box. The bear shook its head and ran. He called Beauty, who ran across the stage and grabbed the bear by the seat of the red diaper it wore. Lafayette waited while Beauty dragged the bear back. Then the magician turned to prepare the box. The bear picked up a book and started to turn the pages.

Lafayette ordered Teddy to put down the book and get back in the box. The bear shook its head. Beauty grabbed the edge of the book in her mouth and tried to pull it from Teddy's hands. The bear clung to the book and stamped its foot angrily.

Lafayette came over and spanked the bear on the seat

of its diaper. He placed the bear in the box. He closed the lid, but reopened it when Beauty barked a warning. The bear had disappeared from the box! While the secrets of this act were never revealed, we can suspect that Lafayette used a vanishing box of the type used to make Beauty disappear in their early vaudeville shows. The act ended with Beauty and Lafayette searching everywhere for the bear.

Teddy was actually a child inside the bear costume.

Lafayette kept his popularity by constantly changing his acts. He never dropped a good one, but found some means to make it better or a little different. Early in his shows he changed David Devant's moth trick into a skit for Beauty. The artist drew a cocoon on a piece of paper stretched on an easel. The paper split and a girl dressed as a moth came out and did a dance. In Lafayette's early version, the magician—dressed as an artist—drew the outline of a doghouse, and Beauty broke through the paper.

Now he made a more elaborate production. He came onstage dressed as a carpenter. He walked to a stand raised several feet off the stage. There was plenty of room under the stand for the audience to see that there was no way anything could enter from a trap door—or so they thought.

Lafayette then built a doghouse on top of the stand. The parts were already cut to size so that they fitted together. But he mysteriously pulled each one of them out of the air.

The first parts were small. He could have taken them from hiding places up his sleeves or in loading pouches in his costume—which is what he did.

However, one of Lafayette's basic tricks was to start out doing a routine in a way that seemed obvious. Then, when smarter members of the audience thought they knew how he was doing the trick, he would pull a switch that completely destroyed the audience's idea of what he had done.

In this case, after producing most of the doghouse parts from his loading pockets, hidden in his workman's coverall, he suddenly pulled the entire roof out of thin air. It was too large to have been hidden anywhere on his body.

Once the doghouse was built, Lafayette stepped out of sight to make one of his lightning changes. He reappeared as himself, waved his wand, and Beauty came out of the doghouse.

The audience had seen the house being built atop the table. The tabletop was so thin that there was no way a secret chamber could have been provided for the dog to hide in before making her appearance. While magicians often hid rabbits in loading pouches in order to appear to pull them out of hats, he could not have done that with an animal as large as Beauty.

So where did she come from? Again, the answer is simple. Beauty got into the empty doghouse the same way she got behind the drawn picture in the earlier act.

She came up through a trapdoor in the floor of the stage. But she did it in a way that masked her from the audience's view. The platform that held the doghouse was high enough off the floor that the audience *thought* it could see under it. But the people in the audience did *not* see under the platform.

A mirror was placed under the table at an angle so that it reflected a view of the floor. This created an illusion that the floor went on under the platform-table. The mirror also masked the sight of Beauty climbing up from under the stage into the doghouse.

This mirror trick has often been used in carnivals to produce bodiless heads, people with the bodies of snakes, and other unusual effects.

Beauty was more than just a performer with the troupe. She had, of course, been credited with saving Lafayette's life. But she was also the watchdog for the show's properties.

Like all magicians, Lafayette had to guard his secrets. While his basic tricks were known to most magicians, some important changes he made were not so well known.

Often minor magicians, or beginners wanting to get started, would try to steal his magical apparatus. Often the thieves were stagehands or assistants to performers who had ambitions to become magicians themselves.

One afternoon before a London matinee, Lafayette was in the basement under the stage. Usually Beauty went with him everywhere he went. The two were rarely separated.

This time Beauty wandered backstage, where the equipment was stored until it was needed on stage. Lafayette had climbed the ladder and was testing the trapdoor to the stage floor. He wanted to make sure that it opened smoothly and with no creaking. This could betray the secret to the audience.

The magician had just pushed the door up when he heard Beauty barking loudly. He came up through the opening as fast as he could, running backstage. He got there just in time to see a stagehand running out the back door, with Beauty in hot pursuit. The man had dropped a notebook and pencil in his hurry.

Lafayette followed the dog. By the time he got to the end of the alley behind the theater, the man had disappeared into the London crowd. Beauty came trotting back, wagging her tail and very pleased with herself. Lafayette gathered her in his arms and took her back to the theater.

An examination of the paper the man had dropped showed that he had been making a drawing of the setup Lafayette used for the Famous Men act. He had hoped to sell the secrets to another magician.

The Famous Men skit was another example of Lafayette's mastery of quick change. He used much the same switch technique as in the Lion's Bride, but it was done so cleverly that the audience never knew that they were seeing the same trickery presented in a different way.

In this act Lafayette propped a huge gilt frame in the middle of the stage. It was deep enough for a man to stand inside. Then the magician hung a black velvet backdrop behind it. He brought out his assistant (the father of the twin boys) and had him stand behind the frame so that his head and shoulders were visible.

He took white greasepaint and covered the black man's face. Next he added a fake mustache and beard. This was followed by a wig. In this way Lafayette slowly built up a living portrait of a famous man of the day. On different days he did different portraits. The most popular with the audience were King Edward VII of England; Lloyd George, the English politician; and the Czar of Russia.

After each portrait was completed, Lafayette walked off the stage. At the instant he did so, the man in the frame removed his wig and beard, and toweled the greasepaint off his face. Then the audience saw that it was not the man they had expected to see. It was Lafayette!

It was simply a matter of clever switches, such as he had used in the Lion's Bride. A mirror under the frame, similar to the one used in the doghouse trick, permitted the original man to get offstage while Lafayette took his place in a brief second during some action planned onstage to divert the audience's attention.

Lafayette was very proud of the way Beauty had protected his secrets. He bragged to all who would listen.

He even said, "If Dr. Watson wrote about Beauty instead of that fellow in his stories, he would tell better tales!"

He was talking about the Sherlock Holmes stories, which were still being written by Sir Arthur Conan Doyle at this time.

Unfortunately, this incident was to have a tragic result. Lafayette now insisted that the backstage doors be locked while his equipment was in the theater. This was dangerous, for if an emergency occurred, there would be no way for those backstage to get out. And an emergency did occur just a few months later. It happened in Edinburgh, Scotland.

After closing a successful London run, Lafayette was booked for a tour of Scotland. His first engagement was a two-week run in Edinburgh. He opened in the Empire Palace Theater on May 1, 1911.

Three days later Lafayette was stunned by the death of his beloved Beauty. She was getting to be very old, but it had never occurred to him that she might die. The end came for the Magic Dog in their room in the Caledonia Hotel. The cause of her death was heart trouble. Lafayette laid the dead dog on a silk pillow and placed lilies around her. Then he knelt beside the dog and wept for his lost friend.

11 * The Last Trick

NO PERSON EVER grieved more for a dead friend than
The Great Lafayette mourned for Beauty. The stage
manager was sure that the magician was in no shape to
put on a show. He put out an order to cancel the performance.

Lafayette, however, was true to the show-business tra-
dition that "the show must go on." The main reason was
that he saw the performance as a memorial to his friend,
partner, and fellow magician.

So that evening, the curtain did not rise on a crowded
stage, as was Lafayette's custom these last few years. The
curtain remained down. The magician walked out in
front of it to face the audience alone.

"My friend, my partner, my fellow magician Beauty is
dead," he told them. "But she has not gone. She is here
with me tonight, as she has been every night since we first
came together twelve years ago. We have not been sepa-

rated in all these years, and I know she has not deserted me now."

The grieving magician, fighting back tears, told how the two of them first worked out their acts. "Our first act was the one where Beauty produces me from a box. The second was the one where she vanishes from a box.

"We have not performed these acts for many years. They are too simple for the kind of show audiences want today. We went on, she and I, to more elaborate and mystifying tricks.

"However, in her honor and as a memorial to my beautiful friend, I want to perform them again tonight. Beauty will be here in spirit. I'll be able to see her and if you look with your heart instead of your eyes, you will see her too. You will see her going through her part of the act as she did twelve years ago when we first began to work together."

Lafayette stepped back behind the curtain. He wiped his eyes and blew his nose. Then he signaled for the curtain to go up. The stage was empty, except for an overturned box that had neither top nor bottom.

Unseen from his position offstage, Lafayette told the audience that Beauty was coming across to the box where she would sit up and wave the wand she carried in her mouth.

Then picking up his Chinese gown and bald headpiece, Lafayette hurried down a ladder into the cellar space below the stage. An assistant pulled a string that the audience could not see. The box fell across the secret trapdoor in the stage floor. Lafayette quickly climbed the ladder, opened the trap door, and appeared as if by magic from the empty box.

Realizing that he had made a mistake, he apologized to the unseen dog and then to the audience. He vanished back down the trap, hastily slipped into the Chinese gown, slapped on his headpiece with its queue, and magically reappeared as Ching Ling Foo.

After completing this act, Lafayette brought out the vanishing box. As he went through the old act, his voice —heavy with grief—described what was happening. His voice and manner were so intense that people in the audience said later that they thought they could actually see Beauty in the box. This was, without doubt, the greatest performance Lafayette ever gave in the twenty-two years he was on the stage.

The next day the magician had a bitter fight with officials of Piershill Cemetery in Edinburgh. He had had an undertaker embalm the body of the dog. Now he wanted Beauty buried in a human cemetery.

Cemetery officials were outraged. They admitted that The Great Lafayette was a peculiar person where the dog was concerned, but this was going too far. Lafayette stormed and raged. Bury Beauty in a pet cemetery? Never! She was human in every way except her form, he insisted. He threatened to hire a lawyer and sue.

He did hire a lawyer, but there was no lawsuit. The lawyer pointed out that there were precedents for beloved pets to be buried with their owners.

Cemetery officials agreed that they would permit this. However, Lafayette wasn't dead yet. One official said very sourly that he would be delighted to bury Lafayette *alive* with the dog!

In the end there was a compromise. They agreed that if Lafayette bought a crypt in the cemetery for himself and signed an order that he would be buried in it upon his death, then the dog's embalmed body could be placed in the crypt to await her master's death.

Even at this stage, Lafayette almost upset the deal. He angrily informed the negotiators that he was *not* Beauty's master. They were friends, partners, and fellow magicians!

Anyway, the agreement was signed. Beauty's body was placed in the crypt. Lafayette went sadly back to his show —and to his own death just five days later.

He seemed to know that his life was drawing to a close. Years before, after Beauty's barking saved him from the lion, Lafayette had said that Beauty was his "luck."

"If anything should happen to her, I will not live long. I was nothing—a third-rate vaudevillian—when she joined me. I will be nothing again when she is gone."

He sincerely believed this. It is shown by the way he acted when he returned from burying his beloved partner. He had his lawyer make arrangements that would provide money for all members of his company should he die suddenly. This money was enough to pay their transportation back to their homes and to help provide for them until they could find another job.

Then he resumed his show, packing the house at each performance. Everyone wanted to see this strange man who loved dogs better than people. They also lined the streets to watch him go to the cemetery after each performance. He did this during the day at the end of the afternoon matinee. He did it again in the dead of night when the evening performance closed. At the cemetery he stood with bowed head for several minutes and then placed a flower in front of the crypt.

People shook their heads and said that the magician was crazy. Perhaps he was rather strange, but people admired him for it.

Beauty died on May 4, 1911. Lafayette died on May 9. There were two shows that night. After the early evening show, there had been a short intermission to clear the house and seat the new audience. The second show proceeded smoothly until about 11 P.M.

Lafayette was presenting as the final act his famous Lion's Bride. This always carried a special thrill for the audiences. Lafayette's publicity agents had spread word of the number of times the magician had almost been killed by a lion used in the act. And, of course, they were aware of the time when the lion escaped during the performance.

Also, there was a special mystery to the act. Everyone knew that Lafayette was a master of quick change, but the way he shifted characters in the Lion's Bride was simply amazing. This long-kept secret was to be revealed upon his death.

The first part of the act went smoothly. The villainous

Pasha, played by Lafayette, told his shuddering young captive that he would have her thrown to the hungry royal lion if she did not marry him. He left her in her room to make her decision.

Then her Persian sweetheart, also played by Lafayette, came riding in on a white horse. He exchanged places with the girl. The audience saw Lafayette put on a bridal gown and cover his head with a heavy veil. He barely got this done before the Turk's slaves came to drag the girl to the lion's cage.

They placed Lafayette, disguised as the bride, in the cage. A set of bars, which could be raised by ropes, separated him from the lion in the adjoining cage.

The Pasha, who everyone knew was Lafayette too, came from the wings to give the signal to raise the bars. Yet Lafayette was under the bride's veil. They had seen him put it on.

Since the Pasha had stepped offstage during the scene when Lafayette came to take the girl's place, it might seem that the Pasha was a double. However, Lafayette cleverly showed that this was not so. When the Pasha ordered the bride thrown into the lion's cage, it was the voice of Lafayette who spoke. This left the audience bewildered. Was the magician in two places at once? Or had he fooled them and not taken the bride's place after all? As if in answer to this doubt, the supposed girl turned away from the Pasha and lifted her veil just enough for the audience to see the face of The Great Lafayette.

At this point there was no more time for the audience

to wonder. The bride was put in the cage. The bars were raised. The lion roared—prodded by the electric shock. The great beast reared up, threw off its false head and The Great Lafayette was revealed as being inside the lion's skin!

This is the way the act usually happened. On this tragic night, a part of the scenery suddenly caught fire during the Lion's Bride act. Flames shot up. Immediately, stagehands began dropping the fire curtain. This is an asbestos curtain fitted behind the regular curtain to protect the audience from fires that started on or backstage. The curtain came almost to the stage and then jammed.

There were three thousand people in the theater. Fortunately, they did not panic. They filed out in an orderly manner, and no one was hurt.

It was a more tragic story backstage. Lafayette, because of the attempts earlier to steal his secrets, always insisted that the back entrances be locked during his performances. Performers and stagehands who were not able to get out across the stage were trapped.

When the Edinburgh fire department finally extinguished the blaze, nine burned corpses were found backstage. One of these was identified as The Great Lafayette. The body was found near that of the horse used in the act. It was thought that he might have saved himself, but turned back to save the horse. He was overcome by smoke and his body partially burned.

Lafayette's body was being prepared for cremation when another body was found in the basement under the stage. It had fallen through when a section of the stage collapsed.

Suddenly there was a new mystery. Lafayette's lawyer identified the new body as that of the magician. The two dead men were very similar in size. The lawyer based his identification upon some rings on the dead man's finger. Then who was the man they had first thought was Lafayette?

Back in America, Houdini heard of the mystery from newspapers. He told reporters, "My friend mystified people when he was alive, and now he mystifies them after he is dead. I envy him!"

The secret, of course, was that Lafayette did use a double. This man, who was the same size as Lafayette, took the magician's place during part of the Lion's Bride act. Lafayette took the part of the Pasha. Then, when the Pasha left the stage, Lafayette did his quick change to the Persian rescuer. The double came back onstage dressed as the Pasha. By this time the real Lafayette had put on the bride's veil and dress. When the Pasha ordered the girl thrown to the lion, he merely waved his hands in the air and opened and closed his mouth. Lafayette, in the bride's costume, spoke the command that the audience heard. Since Lafayette's face was hidden and they saw the mouth of the Pasha opening and closing, it appeared that it was the Pasha who shouted.

The lion's portion of the cage was mounted on a turntable. There was an exact duplicate of the lion's cage on the back that the audience could not see.

A disturbance was created by the Pasha to draw the audience's attention to him for a second. This was long enough for Lafayette, in the bride's gown and veil, to duck behind a piece of conveniently placed scenery. A girl member of his company, similarly dressed, quickly took his place.

Lafayette ran around the back of the scenery. He threw off his veil and gown. He wore his dress suit under them. He took his place in the duplicate cage, crouching down. The fake lion's skin and head were pulled into place.

Out where the audience could see, the guards grabbed the "bride." There was a struggle that pulled the audience's attention to the guards. This is when the turntable moved around. The lion in its cage was carried behind the scenery. The duplicate cage with Lafayette crouched under the head and skin came into place. The girl was then thrown into the adjoining cage and the bars between them lifted.

The light was dim in the lion's cage. When Lafayette jumped up, it looked to the audience as if a real lion had lunged at the girl. Then he threw off the fake head and skin and was revealed as The Great Lafayette in his dress suit. The bride threw off the veil and was shown as the girl they had first seen in the act.

It was a masterpiece of quick change and deception. Every bit of it depended on split-second timing and diverting the audience's attention when a switch had to be made.

After the right Lafayette was found, the body was cremated and his ashes placed in the tomb with Beauty on Sunday, May 14, 1911.

In his lifetime, Lafayette claimed to have had no real friends, except Beauty. But his death showed differently. The road to Piershill Cemetery was lined with people as an open carriage drawn by four horses carried his ashes to the grave. Newspapers said there were thousands in the crowd. In addition, it took sixty carriages to hold those who followed the hearse to the cemetery.

From America, Houdini sent a wire to Edinburgh arranging for a wreath to be sent to the funeral. A message accompanied the wreath. It said, "To the memory of my friend from the one who gave him his best friend, Beauty."

Afterword

IT IS THE nature of magicians to exaggerate. It is part of their show. Everything they do is greater and grander than anyone else's act. So we cannot always believe all they tell us about themselves. There is no doubt that Lafayette exaggerated some of the stories he told about Beauty.

On the other hand, enough people saw her and left accounts of what they saw to prove that she was truly a remarkable dog. In writing this book I carefully assessed all the stories I found about her. I discarded some as being too farfetched. The ones I used are all things that a well-trained dog could do. I invented nothing except the dialogue, and even that is based on paraphrased accounts told to me or found in various accounts of Lafayette and his dog.

There have been many trained animals in shows, but Beauty seems to have been the only one who professed to be a magician herself. She waved a wand in her mouth and things appeared and disappeared. That is stage magic.

The nearest thing to Beauty in the history of magic appears to have been a horse named Morocco, who lived in England in Shakespeare's time. The horse was owned by a man named Banks. A number of famous writers mention the famous "dancing horse." Shakespeare, Ben Jonson, and Sir Walter Raleigh are among them.

A woodcut published in 1595 shows Morocco dancing on his hind legs. He holds a stick in his mouth in the same way that Beauty held her magician's wand.

Then in 1785 a Dr. Gustavus Katterfelto had a cat who became quite famous. In one of his advertisements, Katterfelto answered those who called him and his black cat sons of the devil:

The idea of him and his Black Cat being Devils arises from the astonishing performances of Katterfelto and his said Cat, which both in the day's and the night's performances are such as to induce all spectators to believe them both devils indeed!—the Black Cat appearing at one instant with a tail, and the next without any. . . .

Unlike Beauty, Katterfelto's cat did not profess to be a magician itself. Its sole trick was to make its tail disappear. We may suspect that Katterfelto had two black cats, one of which was born without a tail. He switched the two so cleverly that his audiences never saw the substitutions.

About the same time in London there was a pig who was trained to answer questions by picking up in its snout or pointing to various letters laid out on the ground. Dogs have often been used for this same kind of trick. Monkeys and birds have been favorites with magicians also. Donkeys and horses often appear with magical groups, and once Houdini brought a full-grown elephant on stage and made it disappear.

However, all of these animals and birds were merely props to be used by the magician himself. So far as I know, Beauty still remains the only animal who was a real magician. At least, Beauty thought she was a magician, and her partner, The Great Lafayette, agreed. So did a lot of people who were fortunate enough to see this wonderful Magic Dog.

Further Reading

Carmichael, Carrie. *Secrets of the Great Magicians*. Milwaukee: Raintree Publishers, 1977.

Edmonds, I. G. *The Magic Brothers: Carl & Alexander Herrmann*. New York: Elsevier / Nelson, 1979.

————. *The Magic Makers: Magic & the Men Who Made It*. New York: Elsevier / Nelson, 1976.

————. *The Magic Man: The Life of Robert-Houdin*. Nashville: Thomas Nelson, 1972.

Fortman, Jan. *Houdini & Other Masters of Magic*. Milwaukee: Raintree Publishers, 1977.

Gilbert, George & Rydell, Wendy. *Great Tricks of the Master Magicians*. Racine, Wis.: Western Publishing Co., 1978.

Lamb, Geoffrey. *Illustrated Magic Dictionary*. New York: Elsevier / Nelson, 1980.

Lovitt, Chip. *Masters of Magic*. New York: Scholastic Book Services, 1979.

Michalski, Martin. *Magic Made Easy*. New York: Elsevier / Nelson, 1978.

Reed, Graham. *Magical Miracles You Can Do*. New York: Elsevier / Nelson, 1980.

———. *Magic for Every Occasion*. New York: Elsevier/Nelson, 1981.

Wayne, Bennett, ed. *The Super Showmen*. Champaign, Ill.: Garrard Publishing Co., 1974.

White, Florence M.. *Escape: The Life of Harry Houdini*. New York: Julian Messner, 1979.

Index

About the Author

I. G. EDMONDS says, "*The Magic Dog* really began when I was a seventeen-year-old cub reporter on my first assignment, which was to interview a magician. From that beginning, I have maintained an interest in stage magic, and over the years have done a number of stories about magic and magicians.

"I became specifically interested in Lafayette and Beauty after meeting a man who had seen them on the stage. I wanted to write a book about them right away, but information was severely limited, and it took several years to find out all I wanted to know."

I. G. Edmonds is the author of *The Magic Brothers: Carl and Alexander Herrmann*; *The Magic Makers: Magic and the Men Who Made It*; *The Magic Man: The Life of Robert-Houdin*; and many other books.

He lives in Cypress, California.